P9-DNC-860

UNDER THE LIGHTS

Also by Abbi Glines

The Field Party Series

Until Friday Night

UNDER THE LIGHTS

A Field Party Novel

BY
ABBI GLINES

Simon Pulse
NEW YORK LONDON TORONTO SYDNEY NEW DELHI

This book is a work of fiction. Any references to historical events, real people, or real places are used fictitiously. Other names, characters, places, and events are products of the author's imagination, and any resemblance to actual events or places persons, living or dead, is entirely coincidental.

SIMON PULSE
An imprint of Simon & Schuster Children's Publishing Division
1230 Avenue of the Americas, New York, New York 10020
First Simon Pulse hardcover edition August 2016

Jacket designed by Jessica Handelman
Interior designed by Mike Rosamilia
The text of this book was set in Stempel Garamond LT.
Manufactured in the United States of America
2 4 6 8 10 9 7 5 3 1
This title has been cataloged with the Library of Congress.
ISBN 978-1-4814-3889-6 (hc)
ISBN 978-1-4814-3891-9 (eBook)

To my daughter, Annabelle. It took fourteen years for your love of reading to bloom, but now that it has there is nothing I enjoy more than seeing you lost in a book. This one is for you. There is a lot of you in Willa. I love you.

—Mom

I Needed to Escape My Reality

CHAPTER 1

WILLA

"Hasn't changed much since you left. Go ahead and unpack. Settle in. I got more work to do up at the house. We'll go in the morning and get you registered for school," Nonna said as the pinched frown on her face that had been there since she picked me up at the bus station an hour ago, only grew more intense. "Don't go nowhere. You hear me? Stay put until I get back."

I managed a nod. I hadn't been able to say more than "thanks" to her since I'd seen her. The last time I'd seen my nonna was two years ago when she'd saved up enough money to come visit us in Little Rock. She was a large part of my life. There had been times in my childhood that when

I thought no one else loved me, I knew she did. Nonna never let me down.

Seeing the obvious disappointment in her gaze now was hard to swallow. But I hadn't expected anything different. It was a look I had gotten used to. I saw it in everyone's eyes these days when they looked at me.

No one believed me. Not my mother, certainly not my stepfather, or the police officer who'd arrested me. Not even my brother. No one. Which meant my nonna wasn't going to believe me either. Sure she'd agreed to take me in when my mother packed my bags and left them for me on the front porch the day I was released from the correctional center I'd spent the last six months in. I had nowhere to go, and calling my mother's mother was the only thing I knew to do. I'd lived with Nonna until the summer I turned eleven. Her home was the only real home I'd ever known.

My mother had finally decided she could take care of me, the child she'd had at fifteen and left with her mother the day she graduated from high school three years later. When my brother, Chance, had been eight, his father had finally married my mother. She wanted to bring me into the family. Problem was, I never really fit. My younger brother was adored by his father, and I seemed to always be in the way. I kept to myself until I turned fifteen and everything started to change.

"Answer me, Willa," Nonna demanded, snapping me out of my thoughts.

"Yes, ma'am," I replied quickly. I didn't want to upset her. She was all I had left.

Nonna's expression softened; then she nodded. "Good. I'll be back soon as my work at the big house is done," she added, then turned and walked away, leaving me in the bedroom that had been mine for the first eleven years of my life. I had been happy here. I had felt wanted here.

But I'd messed that up, too. I was good at messing up. If there was a wrong decision to be made, I managed to make it. I intended to put that in the past. I wanted to get back the girl I had been once. The girl whose grandmother was proud of her. The girl who didn't act out for attention. The attention I had gotten from my mother hadn't been the kind of attention I wanted. In the end I'd lost her. She wanted nothing to do with me. I'd killed any love she had for me.

Once the door closed behind Nonna, I sank down onto the twin bed that was covered in a quilt I knew my nonna had made herself. She loved quilting in her free time. Which wasn't very often. She worked six days a week for the Lawtons. They let her off on Sunday so she could go to church and clean her own house. Which happened to be a cottage on the edge of their property. She'd been the Lawtons' housecleaner and cook for as long as I could remember. My mother had grown up in this house. This room I was in had been hers once too.

Even though I'd been the product of a mistake my mother had made, my childhood here had been a happy one. My nonna had given me the love and protection my teenage mother hadn't known how to give. And then there were the boys. Gunner Lawton and Brady Higgens had been my two best friends. Gunner lived in the big house with his parents and older brother, Rhett. From the time he and Brady had caught me in his tree house playing with his army men when we were four, we had been inseparable. I had been watching the boys for weeks go up into that tree house from my front yard at the cottage. I'd wanted to know what was up there. My curiosity had given me my first real friends.

When I had left with my mother, it was at the time things had started to change with all three of us. I wasn't just one of the guys anymore. I was a girl, and things had begun to get awkward. Back then I had thought I was in love with Brady. He'd been popular and had a smile that once made my heart flutter wildly when directed at me. I thought then he'd be the only boy I'd ever love. I'd left soon after my feelings had started to grow. Now I could hardly remember what either boy looked like. There had been other boys in my life since them. Only one made a mark on me. Only one of them I had loved. Carl Daniels. I thought he'd be my forever. Until he decided that sleeping around with other girls was acceptable when I wouldn't give him my virginity in the back of his car.

He had proven to me that I really couldn't trust anyone. Loving someone meant getting hurt. My mother and Carl had both shown me how vulnerable love could make you. I wouldn't make that mistake again.

It seemed like another lifetime now. Gunner and Brady were the safe-and-happy part of my past that I often dreamed about at night when I needed to escape my reality.

My life here would be very different from the way it had once been. I had made a mistake that I would never truly pay for. The guilt and regret would be my companions throughout my life. And being rejected by your own mother wasn't easy to accept. It was a wound that went so deep I doubted I'd ever get over it.

I stood up and walked over to the mirror and studied myself. My mother's dark blue eyes looked back at me. The straight blond hair that hit just below my shoulders was nothing like her red locks. I imagined I got my hair color from my father. A man I didn't know. She would never even tell me his first name. She never even told my nonna. Once she had said it was because he couldn't be a father to me. She was protecting me and him with her silence. I never understood that. I still didn't.

I reached up and ran my fingers over my bare earlobe. The piercings that once framed my ear were almost all gone now. I'd not been able to wear them in the correctional center. I had gotten used to not having to deal with them, and I didn't desire to put them back. Even without them, I was so different from the girl who had left here six years ago.

The Rest of Them Could All Go to Hell

CHAPTER 2

GUNNER

I continued to glare out the passenger window of my own damn truck. I had drunk two beers. That was it. If Brady hadn't been so busy with his hands all over Ivy Hollis, then he'd have seen I was sober enough to drive myself home.

"How're you getting home? I sure ain't letting you take my truck," I told him, glancing over to see Brady smirk. Asshole.

"West is picking me up. He's gotta take Maggie home anyway," was his obnoxious reply. Since West had hooked up with Brady's cousin Maggie, he'd become a do-gooder like Brady. It could drive a guy to drink.

"You completely messed things up for me with Kimmie.

Can't get a girl in my truck alone if you're driving it." And I was pissed about that.

"You should be thanking me. Do you not remember the drama Kimmie caused you last time you got her alone in your truck?"

He had a point. Shaking her loose wasn't easy. I'd had to make out with Serena in front of her to get her to leave me alone. I just grunted a response. I didn't like it when he was right.

"Whatever," I mumbled.

Brady chuckled, and I didn't have to look at him to know he was grinning. "Who is that?" he asked, all the humor suddenly gone from his voice as he slowed the truck down.

I glanced over at him to see which direction he was looking. Following his gaze, I saw someone walking toward the back of the property. It was so dark outside that I couldn't make out who it was. They were nothing more than a shadowy figure from here.

Shrugging, I leaned back in the seat and closed my eyes. I was exhausted. Maybe Brady was right and I wasn't safe to drive. "It's probably Ms. Ames. You know she works late most of the time," I replied, stifling a yawn.

"Ain't real safe for Ms. Ames to be walking in the dark like that, is it?" he asked.

Brady was a perpetual good guy. I swear sometimes it drove me batshit crazy. "She's been doing it for longer than I've been alive. I think she'll be fine." Ms. Ames was our housecleaner and cook. She was also my mother's stand-in mother in a way. When my mother needed advice or help, she always asked Ms. Ames. I liked her better than my own parents. But then I figured she liked me better than my own parents did, so it was mutual. Since my older brother, Rhett, was my parent's favorite child, Ms. Ames had made it clear I was hers. She was also one tough old lady, and I knew anything that encountered her out in the dark better be prepared to be taken down a notch. She could be fierce. I'd seen her take on more than one battle for me when I was a kid, and she always won.

"Maybe I should stop and go check on her. Make sure she gets home safe." His voice still held that tone of concern.

"If you stop this truck, I'll drive my own ass the rest of the way," I warned him. He was the one who was insistent on driving me. We were almost there now, and my bed was so close. I just wanted to get home. Besides, by the time he got to Ms. Ames, she'd be in her house. Safe. Like she always was.

"You're a little shit," Brady grumbled, and continued on his way to my house. I didn't take offense at his comment. Wasn't the first time I'd been called that. My father referred to me as a little shit often. But when he said it, I knew he meant it. And abhorred it. Abhorred me. Because although I carried the last name of Lawton . . . I wasn't his son. I was just the offspring of one of my mother's many affairs. The man I called Father wasn't my biological father. When my older brother was eighteen months old, my dad had gotten prostate cancer, and although the tumor had been removed, his junk never worked again.

Brady pulled into my spot in our six-car garage and turned off the truck, then tossed me the keys. "Go to bed. West just sent me a text, and they're right behind us. I'm going to go walk out there and meet them."

I wasn't stupid. He was going to go check on Ms. Ames. I nodded and thanked him begrudgingly for getting me home in one piece before heading into the house. Walking past my father's office door, I could hear him on the phone. It sounded like business. He was always working. That had once hurt when he hadn't had time to give me. That all changed the day I overheard him call me a bastard, when I was twelve years old. It had been more of a relief than anything. I didn't want to be like him. His pointless life full of anger and bitterness. Concerned with how the world saw him and the appearance of this family. He was everything I never wanted to be. I hated that man.

I never once blamed my mother for cheating on him.

I'd never seen him show her any affection. She was a trophy on his arm, and that was all. Nothing more. He traveled more than he was home.

Where guys like West thought it was okay to love a girl, I knew better. Love wasn't real. It was a fleeting emotion that confused you, then destroyed you in the end. You couldn't trust people. The moment you loved them, they had the power to hurt you.

No woman would ever touch my heart. I was too damn smart for that. I had loved my mother once, but she'd managed to ignore me—unless she wanted to show me off like a prize pony—most of my life. I had loved my father, too, and sought his approval until I realized one day I'd never earn it. Rhett was his golden child. The son who he bragged about. The son that was his. I knew I was better off without all of them, but that still didn't stop my heart from sometimes aching at what I had missed out on.

My life would be full of adventure. It was my life plan. I would never stay tied down to one girl. I'd travel, see the world, and get the hell out of Lawton. Never love anyone and never get hurt again.

When I reached my room, I glanced back down the hall to my mother's bedroom. She and my father didn't share a room. They never had. At least in my lifetime. Maybe once, when the house was new, they had. I wasn't sure nor did I care to know. Her door was closed, and I knew she wouldn't check to see if I was home safely. Because she didn't care. Neither of them did. The only person who cared about me was me. Sure, I'd like to think Ms. Ames did, but the older I got, the more I disappointed her. It was only a matter of time before she hated me too.

I was okay with that. I knew I could always trust myself. That was all I needed. The rest of them could all go to hell.

I Was on a Sinking Ship

CHAPTER 3

WILLA

I was almost back to the cottage from my evening walk to go see if the tree house was still there when I heard leaves crunch behind me. I froze.

"Hey," a male voice called. "What are you doing here? This is private property and that house isn't yours."

My heart sped up as I tried to put the faint memory I had of a young boy's voice to the deeper voice I was hearing behind me. Could it be Gunner? And was I ready to face him?

"You better speak up or I'm calling the police," the guy warned.

I'd seen the headlights coming down the mile-long drive

that led to the Lawtons' house a few minutes ago. They had slowed, and I thought then that I might have to explain myself. I wasn't sure who knew I was back here. Had my nonna told anyone yet? From the sound of his voice, I was thinking my presence was still a secret.

The door opened to the cottage and my nonna appeared. Our eyes met, and then she glanced over my head to the guy behind me. I saw her face soften before she smiled. "Thank you, Brady, for watching out for me, but Willa belongs here. She's moved back to live with me for a while. You remember Willa. Y'all played together as kids."

Brady Higgens. I wished I could remember his face more clearly. The only feeling that I did remember was the flutter in my stomach when he was near me. Slowly I turned around to see the kid from my youth who had played such an important part.

The soft glow from the porch light touched his face, and my breath caught a little. The beautiful boy I'd left behind was tall, muscular, and even more perfect than he'd been when we were eleven. His gaze was locked on mine, and I couldn't seem to form words. I wanted to look away, but then I never wanted to stop looking at him either. It was completely confusing.

"Willa?" His voice was a husky sound that made me shiver.

I nodded. I didn't trust myself to speak just yet. All those silly butterflies he'd caused as a kid were back and more intense.

A smile broke across his face as he took a step toward me. He looked happy, pleased, and something else. Something that I understood. Something that as much as I liked it, I knew I couldn't act on it—he looked interested.

"Willa, come on inside, now." Nonna's voice was stern and held no room for argument. "Thank you again, Brady, for checking up on me. You get yourself home now so Coralee don't worry about you."

I tore my gaze off him and hurried up the steps, keeping my head down so I wouldn't have to meet my nonna's eyes. She had noticed that look in his eyes too. And she didn't trust me. No one did.

If Brady only knew, he wouldn't have looked at me that way.

"Anytime, Ms. Ames. Y'all have a good night," he called out. I kept walking to the bedroom that belonged to me.

I didn't want to hear the lecture to stay away from Brady that I knew was coming. When the front door clicked shut, I cringed and grabbed for my bedroom door.

"Not so fast." Nonna's voice stopped me, and I wanted to growl in frustration. I didn't need her to tell me what I already knew. "Brady Higgens is a good boy, Willa. He's turning into a fine young man. He is quarterback of the football team, and college scouts are already trying to recruit him. He'll make this town proud. You've seen more than that boy has. You know more about the world than he does. He sees that you've turned into a beautiful young woman. That's all he knows. I don't intend on telling folks what happened with you. Ain't their business. But until . . . until you heal from this—until you're better—boys aren't something you need to be spending your time on."

It was hard to hear. Nonna had taken me in when no one else wanted me, but she didn't trust me or believe me either. That hurt. So much so that my chest ached. All I could do was nod. "Yes, ma'am," I replied before hurrying into my bedroom and closing the door to any more hurtful words that she might say. I just needed someone to ask me what had really happened and believe me when I told them.

Just like every night since the accident that changed my life . . . I didn't get much sleep.

Registering for a new high school your senior year was intimidating. Nonna reassuring the principal and counselor that I would cause no trouble had only added to it. I was required to go to the counselor every Tuesday and Friday during my last-period class to discuss how I was feeling. I knew I should be thankful that was the only thing I had to do, but I dreaded it all the same.

Nonna had squeezed my arm and looked me firmly in the eyes while she told me to work hard and make her proud. If she only knew that was exactly what I intended to do. I'd lost too much at this point to lose her, too. I was going to earn her trust. I had to.

The first bell had already rung while I was meeting the counselor and Nonna was explaining my situation. Which meant I was going to have to walk into my first period of the day late. Everyone would stare at me. The teacher would stop talking, and he would also stare at me.

I glanced down at my schedule. Mr. Hawks was my US Government teacher, and I'd be facing him first. I walked down the empty hallway lined with lockers until I found room 203. I could hear who I assumed was Mr. Hawks talking through the door. Taking a deep breath, I reminded myself that I had faced things far scarier than this. I had lived through six months with girls who deserved to be in a correctional facility. That had been truly terrifying. This was just a classroom of kids who would never understand me. Who didn't matter. All that mattered was that I made the best grades I could and stayed completely out of trouble.

My hand touched the cool metal of the door handle, and I twisted it before I could delay this any longer and entered the room. Just as I predicted, every eye swung toward me. I didn't make eye contact though. I kept my gaze on the balding older man in the front of the room with a button-up shirt on that barely covered his belly.

"You must be Willa Ames," he said with a smile that didn't meet his eyes. "Please take a seat, Willa. We were just going over last week's notes. There will be a test on them two days from now. I will expect you to ask a fellow classmate for a copy of their notes and prepare yourself. No time like the present to get caught up with the lessons. Just be careful whose notes you ask for. Not everyone in here is a passing student." He finished that last bit by scanning the room as he looked over his half-moon glasses.

"Yes, sir," I replied before turning to go to the only empty desk in the room. I didn't look at anyone around me. I kept my gaze focused on that desk like it was a raft and I was on a sinking ship.

The Tree House Looks the Same

CHAPTER 4

GUNNER

"What made you decide to mess with crazy? Thought you'd had your fill of that already?" West Ashby asked me as we walked out of first period. It was the only class we had together. Other than being a great running back, he was also brilliant. Most of the classes he took were advanced classes. I couldn't figure out why he did it. He'd go to college on a football scholarship. It wasn't like he needed an academic one too.

"Not sure what you're talking about," I replied.

"Kimmie, man. She's telling everyone y'all hooked up and are back together. From the way I remember, y'all were never together."

Kimmie? Seriously? I hadn't even slept with her, and she was telling shit. Maybe I did owe Brady a thank-you for hauling my ass home last night. "She's lying."

West chuckled. "Then you better straighten that out with her. Because she's standing at your locker looking like a lovesick puppy."

I jerked my head up and looked over at my locker. Sure enough. There stood Kimmie, smirking at me.

"Shit," I grumbled.

"You're gonna have to get a restraining order on that one," West replied in an amused tone.

I needed to get to my locker, but I didn't need to that badly. I headed down the hall for my second period.

"Good luck," West called out behind me. I wasn't in the mood for his humor.

I hadn't gotten very far before a hand wrapped around my arm. "You aren't even going to come see me? I was waiting on you!" Kimmie's chipper voice grated on my nerves.

"Let go of my arm," I demanded through my clenched teeth.

"But I wanted to talk to you. After last night I figured we had a lot to talk about," she continued as if I hadn't asked her to let me go.

I glanced over her head and saw the sign for the girls' restroom. Before this got any more embarrassing, I shoved her toward the door, then opened it and went inside, knowing she would have to follow me if she was going to keep ahold of my arm.

She began to giggle. "Bad boy, going in the girls' restroom."

I dropped my books on the edge of the sink, then reached over and detached Kimmie's hold on me. "What the fuck is wrong with you?" I asked, stepping away from her once I was free. "I was drinking. We made out a little. Hell, I don't remember most of it." Okay so that was a lie. I was not drunk. Just being stupid.

Kimmie looked as if I'd slapped her. "But I thought that you wanted to get back together. I thought you liked me."

I let out a frustrated sigh. "Kimmie. I don't do girlfriends. Everyone in this school knows that. We were never together. We hooked up. That was it."

Her bottom lip began to quiver, and I wanted nothing more than to grab my books and get the hell out of here.

"But—but—I thought—" she began to stammer.

"You thought wrong. But I will make you a promise. I'll never come near you again. Drunk or sober. So back off and leave me alone."

Kimmie let out a sob and covered her mouth, then ran for the door. I knew this time I'd just had to be straightforward. The last time she thought we were an item I had tried being nice and letting her off easy. But she'd started showing up at my house with food and stalking me. I had used Serena to show her that we were not a couple. I wasn't in the mood to do something that drastic again.

I reached for my books just as a door to one of the stalls opened. I had thought we were alone. Smirking, I waited to see who had overheard all this. Hopefully, it was someone with a big mouth so that the rumors that I was dating Kimmie would be squashed before lunch.

One long, very tan, smooth leg stepped out. The girl was wearing some beat-up Chucks, which didn't take away from that leg. . . . Damn that was a nice leg. I let my gaze travel up until shorts finally ended the endlessly long leg and the rest of her appeared.

Who the hell was she?

Blue eyes the color of the sky framed by thick black eyelashes stood out on her heart-shaped face. They were studying me closely, as if she wasn't sure just what she thought of me. I quickly took in the rest of her face, full pink lips, and a perfect little nose. All in a halo of blond hair that was almost too pale to be real.

"When did you become so cruel, Gunner Lawton?" The southern drawl in her voice was smoother than those I heard around here. It had more of a musical sound. One that you could listen to for days and never get tired of.

Wait . . . she knew me. I stopped memorizing her mouth and lifted my gaze to meet hers. Who was she? I'd remember her. There was no way I had ever met her.

"You don't know who I am, do you?" she asked, and her mouth curled up into a crooked little grin. "Figures. It's been a while. However, I knew who you were the moment I saw you. Your voice is deeper now . . . but your eyes are the same."

I had to shake out of this trance. She was just a girl. A seriously smoking-hot girl, but she wasn't going to have this crazy effect on me. "Can't say I remember you," I finally responded.

She let out a small laugh as she washed her hands and looked at me in the mirror. "It's okay. Brady didn't recognize me either," she said, then dried her hands on a paper towel. She walked toward the door and tilted her head to the side as she stopped beside me. "The tree house looks the same" was all she said before she walked out the door.

The tree house . . . Brady . . . Holy shit! That was Willa Ames.

That Was Completely on Purpose

CHAPTER 5

WILLA

They had turned out much like I expected. Gunner had always been cocky and sure of himself. He hadn't been cruel as a kid, but I wasn't surprised at what I had overheard. Beautiful Gunner Lawton ruled this town. He had money and the power of his family name, and he was breathtakingly gorgeous.

But he didn't give me butterflies back then. Not one. That was all apparently just for Brady. Figures I'd get butterflies over the good guy who would never accept me once he knew my past. The truth behind why I was back in Lawton. My nonna would make up some lie, and everyone would believe it. I'd have to go with it if I wanted to stay here.

"Willa Ames." Gunner called out my name, and I smiled. It hadn't taken him long to figure it out.

Glancing back over my shoulder, I saw him walking toward me with a grin on his face that said everything I knew he was thinking. "Go wipe that girl's tears and be nice," I replied, but I waited on him to catch up to me.

He rolled his eyes. "You have no idea the crazy that I was dealing with in there."

Of course it wasn't his fault. Never was. Gunner always had a reason why he wasn't wrong. "So your penis accidentally fell into her vagina?" I asked in a mocking tone.

He chuckled. "No, that was completely on purpose. Damn you look good. When did you move back?"

He was over talking to the poor girl in the restroom. Maybe now she would be smarter in her next choice in a guy. Gunner wasn't a choice. He was a fun time. "Nonna picked me up at the bus station yesterday."

"So you're living with Ms. Ames again? When were you planning on coming to say hello?"

I hadn't been. Nonna didn't want me at the big house. I knew that without her even saying it. So I shrugged. "It's been six years." That wasn't a real answer, but it was all I had.

Gunner cocked one eyebrow. "And?" was his response.

"And I knew we would see each other at school. Wasn't sure how you had turned out, or if our childhood friendship would carry into our teen years."

Gunner looked me up and down like he had in the restroom. "I'm a guy, Willa. We can be friends or something else. Just whatever you might be up for."

It was my turn to roll my eyes. That was the silliest come-on I'd ever heard. And I'd heard a lot of them.

"I'm up for making it to my next class on time and staying out of trouble. It was good to see you again, Gunner. I'm sure we will run into each other again. Small town, small school and all," I replied, then turned and left him standing there in that hallway. Encouraging anything between us was wrong and pointless.

I didn't make eye contact with anyone else as I made my way to room 143. I had to prove to Nonna I was worth it. I'd be the easiest teenage girl in the world to raise. I wasn't giving her any problems. Besides, I'd done enough already to last a lifetime. No more regrets. I had my fair share.

A tall guy with the clearest blue eyes I'd ever seen caught my attention before I heard Gunner's voice call out "Nash," and his gaze left me. "Yeah," he replied.

I didn't wait around for an introduction. Gunner was trouble. He had no regrets. I did. I just hoped he never had regrets like mine, ones that were nearly unbearable to live with. We weren't invincible. I'd learned that a little too late.

High school was the same everywhere, or at least inside the United States. No one got real original. You had the same groups, same silliness, and same stupidity. The only difference here was no one knew me. The kids I'd gone to school with as a child had forgotten me, and the two boys who did remember me weren't telling everyone else who I was. In fact, Brady went as far as ignoring me in the one class we had together.

That in itself had been disheartening. He had sat beside a pretty brunette girl and a guy who she must be dating. They were very touchy. Brady made jokes with them and acted like I wasn't there until class was over and he nodded his head with a simple hello on his way out the door.

For a moment I wondered if he had somehow heard what I had done. Not that it mattered. I wasn't trying to get his attention. I had no time for butterflies and the like. My life would exist to make my nonna proud and to one day maybe get my brother to speak to me again. My mom could suck a lemon, and I never wanted to see my stepfather again.

So that was my life. I had made my bed, and now I

would have to lie in it. My nonna had said as much when she picked me up from the bus station.

"How was school?" Nonna asked, walking out of the small kitchen in her house while wiping her hands on an apron tied around her waist.

Replying *It sucked balls* probably wouldn't go over real well. So I went with "Good." For her benefit only.

She didn't look convinced. "Put your book bag in your room and come help me with peeling the potatoes for the dinner at the big house tonight."

Nonna usually did all the preparing of the food for the big house at the Lawtons' house. My being here had brought her home for the afternoon. To check on me. It felt good to be cared about. That wasn't something I was used to anymore.

"Yes, ma'am." I would do whatever I needed to stay here. I never wanted to go home, even if my mother allowed it.

I left my book bag on my bed and slipped off my Converse before going back to the kitchen in my socked feet. Six nights a week Nonna made dinner for the Lawtons. Saturday night was normally a big night when she had to cook for the guests Mrs. Lawton would entertain. Many times it was a party, and Nonna had to hire in help. Sundays the Lawtons went to dinner at the country club in Franklin, Tennessee, that was an hour drive away. Although Gunner used to not go and would stay with us after he had made his appearance at the Baptist church with his parents.

I was sure that had all changed. Gunner probably spent his Sundays with friends, going to the field parties we used to anticipate being involved in one day. In a small town like Lawton, there wasn't much to do on the weekends, so the field parties were the one place all the teens could go to have a good time. It was a tradition among the popular at Lawton High. After what I saw today, there was no question in my mind that Gunner and Brady were pack leaders in that elite group.

"Grab a peeler. I'll use the knife. Don't need you cutting a finger off," Nonna said when I walked into the kitchen. There was a large tub of washed white potatoes to be peeled.

I did as I was told and began peeling a potato over the hand towel she had laid out for me.

"How was your classes?"

My mother had never once asked me about my classes. She didn't ask me much of anything. I had forgotten how much I missed knowing someone cared. Leaving Nonna had been the hardest thing I'd ever done.

"The truth? Boring."

Nonna made a tsking sound. "Need school to make it in life."

I understood that, but the classes were going over things I already knew. I had been in advanced classes before being sent to the correctional center. "I know. I'll make good grades," I assured her.

She dropped a peeled potato in the bowl of water and reached for another. "Did you see Gunner or Brady?"

As if I wouldn't see them in that small high school. "Yes, ma'am. I have classes with both of them."

"Did you speak to them?"

"Yes, ma'am. Not much though." I knew she was worried about my being involved with either of them. She didn't trust me, and why should she? I had done nothing to earn anyone's trust.

"You'll make friends soon enough. Just pick good ones, though. You are who you spend time with. Guess you learned that lesson the hard way already."

Yes, I had. A lesson I wish I'd never had to learn. I had spent hours, days, and weeks wishing I hadn't been there that night. That I had been smart. That I hadn't seen what I'd seen.

"Your momma ain't perfect—Lord knows that. But she tried to bring you into her home and be the mother she had failed at being the first part of your life. You can't go blaming her or anyone else for what you did. You made them mistakes and now you got to pick up and figure out life again."

I didn't need to be told that I made my own mistakes. I lived with that daily. However, Nonna thought my mother tried to be a mom to me. She hadn't. Not really. I often wondered why she'd sent for me six years ago. I had never been able to make her happy. Now the one woman who had loved me thought I was a loser of the worst sort.

If I did anything else in this life, it would be making my nonna proud of me again. I didn't care if I ever saw my mother again though. When I had needed her most, she hadn't listened to me. She hadn't believed me. No one had.

Call It Whatever You Want

CHAPTER 6

BRADY

Maggie's bedroom door was open when I walked up the stairs. I knew her boyfriend, who was also one of my best friends, had gone with his mother to a counseling session after workouts today. Since his father's death a couple months ago, his mother had been in and out of town, going back to her parents' house. They weren't the same after losing his dad. His mom wasn't handling it well at all.

Maggie's dark hair hung over her shoulder, blocking her face as she looked down at the book she was reading in her hands. I cleared my throat, announcing my presence. She jerked her head up, and her expressive eyes went wide. Then she smiled. "Oh, hey, Brady."

My cousin didn't speak at all when she'd first moved in with us. I had West to thank for her actually saying my name, or anything for that matter. When she had held his hand and been his strength while he watched his father die of cancer, he had given her a reason to speak again.

"What are you reading?" I asked, walking into her room, which had once been my room.

"*Voyage in the Dark* by Jean Rhys."

I had no idea what that was. Figures Maggie wasn't reading something I had heard of. She wasn't a *Twilight*-reading kind of girl. I nodded like I knew what the hell she was talking about.

She smirked. "A young girl with a dead father and bitchy stepmother. But she's not Cinderella."

"Ah, okay."

She laughed at my response. "Are you bored? Why the visit?"

I rarely stopped by her room. But then she was rarely alone. West was either here, or she was there. Figured I'd get to the point. She wasn't one for chitchat. "Do you have any classes with the new girl?"

She raised her eyebrows. "Willa Ames? Yes, we both have a class with her, together." Oh yeah . . . I'd forgotten she and West were even in the room. I'd been so busy watching Willa and not getting caught that I couldn't focus on anything else. I had wanted Willa to speak to me, but she hadn't spoken to anyone.

"I mean any other classes with her?" I corrected my minor mistake.

Maggie set her book down and turned to fully look at me. "West told me she was really close to you and Gunner when y'all were kids. And you couldn't stop watching her in class. Do you like her? Is that what this is about? Because I'm fairly certain if you want her, you can turn on your charm and get her."

She didn't know Willa very well, but then neither did I. Not anymore. She was different. Not just her looks, because like everyone else she'd grown up. She wasn't the little girl with pigtails and dirty knees from playing ball with us anymore. It was more than that. She was harder, withdrawn, and untouchable. The carefree, laughing girl I once knew was gone. Completely.

"She's changed. I'm curious."

Maggie shrugged. "Call it whatever you want. But you're more than curious. It was entertaining to watch."

This was a pointless conversation. "Whatever" was my annoyed response before I turned and walked back out the door. I loved my cousin, but she wasn't a normal girl either. She wasn't going to be much help in all this.

"She watched you, too, when you weren't looking,"

Maggie called out, and I paused. A smile slid over my lips that I couldn't control.

"Thanks," I replied without turning around, then made my way to my attic bedroom.

Before Willa had moved away to live with her mother, things had gotten awkward with the three of us. Gunner and I both had become attracted to her. Days before we found out she was moving, he and I had made a pact that neither of us would ever ask her to be our girlfriend. We would always just be best friends. Nothing more.

It seemed silly now. Gunner and I competed for girls and on the field all the time. The days of us being friends first were long gone. Gunner was my friend, but he was also a spoiled jerk a good portion of the time. His parents sucked, but he did have every materialistic thing he so desired. That got annoying.

But back then he'd been one of the best friends I'd had, and I hadn't wanted to lose that. Not even over a girl. Neither had Gunner. We'd been determined to stay close no matter what. Things sure had changed.

Willa hadn't been our first big fight. Serena had when we were in the eighth grade. Before we figured out Serena would make her way through the whole football team before sophomore year.

I wondered how well that would have worked out if

Willa had stayed. Would she have been our first big fight? Would we have lost our friendship over her? Because even though we were kids, we both loved her. That much I knew was true. She wasn't that girl now though. The darkness in her eyes said things in her life had changed. She was different. And I wanted to know why.

"Brady!" Maggie's voice carried up the stairs leading to my room. I paused at the top step and turned to look down at her. She'd followed me.

"Yeah?"

Maggie bit her bottom lip nervously, then sighed before speaking again. I waited.

"I see something in her eyes that I recognize. There is hurt there. The deep kind of pain that changes you. The girl you once knew probably isn't there now. She's different. Something has happened to her. But she does watch you. She doesn't watch Gunner that way. She was in three of my classes today, and not one time did she pay attention to anyone the way she did you. Just . . ." She paused and gave me a sad smile. "Be careful with her."

I wasn't sure how I liked my cousin warning me not to hurt someone. I wasn't that guy. "What do you think I'm going to do to her?" The question came out annoyed because I was.

Maggie's frown became pinched. "Ivy Hollis. Last I checked you were dating her." Then she turned her all-knowing, haughty ass around and walked away.

Well damn. I guess she was right. I couldn't get to know Willa and keep my weird relationship with Ivy. But I didn't want to hurt Ivy, either.

A car door slammed outside, and I glanced out the window to see West walking up the sidewalk. He didn't look happy, but then he never was after these counseling visits with his mother. The first thing he always did was run to Maggie. I had worried about him using her in the beginning, but she needed him just as much. They had both lived through pain I'd never known. It bonded them. I loved them both, and I was thankful they had each other.

I didn't have that kind of loss in my life. The darkness haunting Willa's eyes I didn't recognize. Could I ever be the shoulder she needed to lean on? If I didn't have my own demons to conquer how could I help her?

Ivy was easy. We understood each other. We were alike in many ways. A relationship with her was comfortable. She was sweet and dependable, if not also annoying at times. If I even mentioned I wanted something for lunch, the next day she'd bring it. When I complained about my locker being a mess and not being able to find anything, she organized it for me after school as a surprise. She cared about me. A lot. I didn't have to work to make her happy. Even if I knew I didn't love her.

Was that what I wanted? Easy? Or did I want more?

Still One Big Happy Family

CHAPTER 7

GUNNER

Family dinner was a fucking joke. If Mom wanted me there, then she was going to be disappointed. Grandmother Lawton could equally kiss my ass. I didn't give a shit if a woman who I shared no blood with was in town. It was Rhett she always cared about seeing anyway, and he only came home from college during the Christmas holidays. Dinner with people who didn't care if I was breathing wasn't on my to-do list. I had other plans. Something I'd been planning all day. I was going to see Willa.

Ms. Ames would be serving the family dinner, and I'd have Willa alone. All that closed-off shit she was throwing today at school wasn't going to fly with me. She was back. I was curious as hell. And she was smoking damn hot. That smart mouth asking me if my penis had accidentally fallen into Kimmie's vagina had been hilarious and exactly the kind of comment I expected from the Willa I knew.

I knew a different Willa. One that Brady didn't know. She had never really been herself around Brady. She had been giggling and blushed a lot when he was around. I was young, but I'd known even back then what that meant. Where she would tell me jokes and laugh until her side hurt and she snorted, she wasn't so free around Brady. Because I was her friend. She wanted more from him.

And I was so damn jealous back then I'd not been able to see straight. Willa was mine. I didn't want to share her with Brady, but I had because he was my best friend. When I realized she liked him differently than me, I remember my young heart breaking. I already didn't have my parents' love. They adored Rhett. Then Willa had chosen Brady. It was in her eyes. I knew the sting of rejection too well at that point. I swore if I lost her to Brady, I'd never love anyone else again. I would only love me. I trusted me. She'd left before that happened though. I never really lost her to Brady, but somehow I'd still built walls around me. Maybe it was because her leaving had hurt too bad and I never wanted to experience that again.

I didn't use the front door. Not because I was afraid of being caught. I really didn't give a shit if my mom caught me leaving. I just didn't want anyone to know I was headed to Ms. Ames. I wanted to talk to Willa alone.

I escaped out of the door farthest from the pre-dinner drinks in the living room. Mom had called for me twice now, and I expected another summons soon. I'd be gone by then. When Ms. Ames came looking for me, she'd be upset with me, but I knew deep down she'd understand. I figured Ms. Ames was well aware that by blood I was no Lawton. She'd been here before I was born.

I climbed up in my truck and headed out to the main road in case anyone was watching me leave. I didn't want them to figure out I had gone to find Willa. I had no doubt my mother would frown upon that one. She'd never approved of our friendship when I was younger. I heard at least three times a week that Willa was the help's kid and not someone I should be spending so much time with.

Once she had told Ms. Ames the exact same thing, and Willa had been kept from me for a week. I'd refused to eat or speak to my mother. She'd then decided that had been a bad idea and allowed me back my friend. But she still didn't approve. Which might have been another reason I wanted to be around her so much.

Pulling behind Ms. Ames's cottage, I hid my truck from

the view at my house. I had watched Willa all day, and not one damn time did she look my way after that smart little comment in the hallway. I waited to see if she talked to Brady, but they hadn't even spoken to each other. At least it didn't seem like it when I saw them both in the halls. When Brady had actually walked past her and not said a word and Willa had glanced his way, I'd almost gone after his ass. He should have said something to her.

We had been close once. Willa had only ever really had us as a kid. She was the help's granddaughter, so no one really invited her to birthday parties or to play. Only Coralee ever had Willa over. Brady was the only other person she really knew here. This had to be hard on her, coming back and leaving the life she'd made for herself in Little Rock. Where was his sensitivity? He normally carried it around on his shoulders like a princess.

I hadn't even made it halfway to the door when it opened, and Willa stepped out onto the small back porch. She didn't look happy to see me. Not that I expected her to be thrilled, but she had to be in need of a friend after today. She was a girl after all. Didn't they need friends to talk to? Sure she hadn't been girly back in the day, but she was all girly-looking now.

"I'm not doing your book report, nor am I going to steal cookies out of the kitchen for you," she said as she propped her hip against the door frame and crossed her arms over her chest. Thank God she was wearing a bra. I wasn't sure I'd be able to control my reaction to her if she'd been that comfortable.

"Damn," I replied to her, unable not to grin. "And I was sure I'd get those chocolate chip cookies while you did all my homework. What happened to you, Willa? You've changed." I was teasing, but then I wasn't. I did want to know what had caused the lightness in her eyes to darken and fade.

She shrugged. "I realized I was being used for my nonna's cookies and my brain, so I moved on."

Having her back was odd. I used to lie in bed at night and imagine what it would be like if she came back. But those days were long gone. It had taken me months to get over the ache of her leaving. Brady had even teased me about being lovesick. It had made me mad at him for not missing her like I did when he had been the one she wanted. He had her love and didn't even realize it.

"There's a family meal going on up at the big house. I peeled potatoes, chopped up broccoli, and rolled up fancy cheese in fancy meat for over three hours this afternoon. You should be up there eating it. What will your mother think?" She was mocking my mother with her proper tone.

"She'll bitch and moan and apologize to my old-as-fuck

grandmother; then she won't speak to me for a week. It'll be heaven and worth it all."

A smile broke across her face, and I swear my heart skipped. Damn.

"Nothing has changed in the Lawton house, I see."

I shook my head. "Nope. Not a thing. Still one big happy family. Except Rhett's off at college now and I'm left to suffer through hell alone."

At the mention of happy family her smile faded and her shoulders lost some of their bravado. She was hurting. I knew that already. I just wish I knew why.

"Gotta love those fairy-tale lives. Must be nice." I knew she wasn't accusing me of having one. She knew how badly my family sucked. Her more than anyone.

"Sure you don't want to share some of Nonna's cookies with me? I'm missing dinner with that lovely family to see you. At least you could feed me."

She shoved off from the door frame and nodded her head toward the kitchen inside. "I guess. Come on, and I'll feed you a healthy meal of peanut butter cookies and whole milk like only my nonna can supply."

It had been a while since I'd had her nonna's cookies. My mother didn't allow anything as terrible as sweets in the house, and I was too old to come begging Ms. Ames for a treat. Not to mention, the idea of coming to this house and not seeing Willa had been too hard for so long it had become a habit to stay away from here. Even after time healed my broken eleven-year-old heart.

Following her into the house, I watched her ass twitch. It was a really nice ass. Hard not to look at, and I wasn't going to not look while I had the chance.

"I think she has lemon pound cake, too. Want to add that to your healthy dinner of cookies and milk?"

"Hell yeah. I'm a growing boy."

She let out a soft laugh and shook her head. "I'd offer you a sandwich, but I doubt you'll have room for it with all the baked goods."

"Cookies and cake are just fine. So how did you like school today? Suck here as bad as your last school?"

I doubted anyone loved school. I was going to get her talking about her past and why she was back, but I needed to trick her into it.

"Looks like you love school just fine." She sounded snide as she pulled a frozen glass mug out of the freezer, then filled it with milk. I'd forgotten that Ms. Ames froze her milk glasses. That always made the milk taste better somehow.

"Are you being a smart-ass again?" I asked, torn between watching the icy cold milk with anticipation and the way her body looked in that outfit.

"Stating a fact isn't being a smart-ass," she replied as she turned to bring my milk and cookies over to me. I liked the way her voice had that raspy tone in it. Her drawl wasn't as thick as it had once been, but it was there.

Lingering.

I Just Want Out of Here

CHAPTER 8

WILLA

Inviting Gunner in was probably stupid. His mother would hate it if she found out. Nonna would be furious. And Gunner wasn't exactly friend material anymore. He was everything a wealthy, spoiled, good-looking guy turned out to be.

But I'd let him in. Because I was lonely maybe. Because I needed company from someone who didn't look at me with disappointment. Because for now I didn't want to think about what I'd done wrong, or the correctional hell I'd lived through. Or the fact my mother hated me.

So here I was with Gunner Lawton in my nonna's kitchen, eating cookies and pound cake and drinking milk, when I knew he should be at his family dinner with the all-important Grandmother Lawton. The boy I used to know, however, wasn't one to upset his mother. He tried to make his dad happy. I poured myself a glass of milk too and joined him at the table.

"When did you decide to become a rebel and piss off the folks? Is this a new thing, or have you been at it awhile now?" I asked, truly curious.

Gunner looked at me over the frosty glass he was taking a drink out of. I could see anger flash there, then a coldness. He was different all right. I wasn't the only one who had changed. I guess we all did that with age and time.

"Stopped giving a shit what they wanted a few years back" was the only response I got.

"No more cotillion events then?" I asked, not even trying to hide my smirk. He had hated the cotillion his mother made him attend back when we were younger. He'd even begged her to let him take me once so he wouldn't have to dance with one of those country club girls in their long white dresses and fancy hats.

"Fuck no. God those were terrible," he said with a grin tugging at his lips. He had really good lips.

"Little Gunner Lawton always tried to please his momma and did all he could to get his dad's approval. Guess I didn't expect that to change with puberty." I was pushing him. But I liked thinking about his past instead of mine.

Gunner finished off his lemon pound cake before looking back up at me. I could see the indecision in his eyes. There was something there. He wanted to tell me, but he wasn't sure if he should. His expression had always been so telling. Lying when we were younger was never his thing. Brady had been able to call him out on his shit with ease. As had I.

"I don't want to be my parents. I don't want their life. Maybe Rhett does. I just want out of here" was what he finally said. But it wasn't what he was hiding. That was still there in his eyes. I wasn't going to push though. If he tried to find out why I was here, he wouldn't get that answer either. I understood secrets and his need to have his own.

"Why are you back?" His question wasn't even hesitant.

I knew this was coming. I expected it.

"Made some stupid choices and Mom kicked me out." That was as honest as I was going to be.

Gunner leaned back in his chair, crossing his arms over his chest as he studied me. He thought he knew me well. He had no idea how much he didn't know now. "Drinking? Weed? Sex? Which one was it? Or was it harder shit?"

I stood up, taking my glass with me. I would need to wash it and put it back in the freezer before Nonna got home and saw two glasses dirty. She didn't need to know Gunner had been here. I knew she wanted me to keep my distance, but it had been Gunner who came to me. I hadn't sought him out.

"Leave it at that," I said, walking over to take his empty glass and crumb-covered plate.

"All three?" he asked, raising his eyebrows as if he was impressed. God he was so naïve. Nothing about my story was impressive. It was life changing but not in a good way.

"You want to tell me why you suddenly decided impressing your folks wasn't important?" I snapped back, glaring at him in warning. He closed down. All expression from his face void. That's what I thought.

"Exactly," I replied. "Same with me. Let's leave it be."

Gunner sighed, then nodded. "Okay. Fair enough."

Hell yeah it was fair enough. He had secrets and so did I. We both would have to deal with those secrets and what was eating us up inside alone. The friendship we once had where we told each other everything was that of children. Our secrets now were bigger. More important.

When my feelings were hurt or I had a nightmare that bothered me, I told Gunner. Never Brady. I didn't want Brady to think I was a baby. But Gunner I trusted to be there no matter what. He and I had a bond that only two kids with parents who didn't want them could have. Brady didn't know what that felt like. But for Gunner and me, it was a reality we lived with. We always knew we weren't alone. We had each other, and that helped through the hardest times.

"Want a ride to school tomorrow?" he asked, standing up.

Was I allowed to ride with him? Nonna probably wouldn't like it. But then she was at the big house when I would have to walk out to the main road to catch the bus. Would she even know I was riding with Gunner?

I wanted to.

Having someone my age to talk to was nice. I missed that.

I was lonely. I had been for over six months.

"Yeah, I would. Thanks."

He grinned. "I'll be by around seven thirty." He nodded outside to the now darkened sky. "Your nonna is probably cleaning up and getting ready to head home. I better go."

"Yeah," I agreed.

"Thanks for the food," he said, then turned and headed outside.

For the first time in a long time I smiled. A real smile. One that I actually felt without the heaviness on my chest that had become a part of me.

I finished cleaning up all evidence of his being here, then went to my bedroom to pick out a book from our required reading list I had been given today. After school I had stopped in the library and grabbed the first three books I found on the list. I was a fast reader. I figured I could knock out this list of fifteen books in a few weeks, even if I was behind.

Escaping into books had been my only relief in life since that night my world changed. I had read anything I could get my hands on while in the correctional facility. Before that I hadn't been much of a reader. I had read Harry Potter and Twilight, but that had been about it for me.

The Great Gatsby, *A Passage to India*, *Under the Volcano*, *Lord of the Flies*, and *Lolita* were all some of my favorites now. One thing I'd learned was good literature was good literature no matter what genre or year it was written. It was the only positive thing that came from my time spent in juvie.

I sat down on my bed, crossed my legs under me, and picked up the copy of *To Kill a Mockingbird*. This was on our list to read for the year, and I figured since I had actually heard of this one, then I'd start with it. The other two I had picked up at the library I wasn't so sure about. *A Town Like Alice* and *1984* would have to wait until I finished this one.

Maybe I'm Not a Good Friend Then

CHAPTER 9

BRADY

Ivy was saying something. I think I heard the words Friday night and maybe something about a party. My attention wasn't on her. Instead it was completely directed at Gunner's fancy-ass truck and the girl climbing out of the passenger's side.

After the way Willa ignored us both yesterday I didn't expect to see her riding to school with Gunner. I wondered if Ms. Ames had set this up. Gunner stopped at the front of the truck and said something to Willa that made her laugh. My chest tightened with what felt like jealousy at the sight, and I felt my hands fist at my sides.

Gunner was making her laugh. She was riding with

Gunner, and now she was talking to him while she smiled. Last night something must have happened to bring the two of them together. They seemed like old friends instead of strangers. They *were* old friends, but so was I. Why wasn't I involved in this little moment of fucking friendship?

"Are you good with that?" Ivy asked, tugging on my arm.

Was I good with what? Gunner and Willa hanging out. No, I wasn't. Why? Well I didn't want to think about that too deeply. However, I didn't think that was what Ivy was referring to. So I replied to her question with "Huh?" and saw her face scrunch up in a frown and quickly added, "Oh, sure." Which made her smile and hopefully shut up with the chattering.

Kimmie and Serena both bombarded Gunner and blocked out Willa in one swift move as if they were operating as a whole and not two parts. I didn't watch to see how Gunner handled it because I was too busy watching Willa roll her eyes, then move on toward the front doors. That made me smile. She wasn't trying to lay any claim, nor did she want to. That was obvious, and I was so relieved I didn't worry about the fact I'd agreed to something with Ivy that I hadn't fully heard.

"Are you coming?" Ivy asked.

I didn't much care for the possessive, bossy way she'd

asked me. So I did the mature thing and started toward Willa. "Nah, I'll see you later," I called back to Ivy without a glance, then hurried to catch up with Willa before she got out of my sight.

Ivy called my name, but I pretended not to hear her and broke into a jog. I was being a jerk. I knew it and I felt bad about it, but my getting to Willa had suddenly become more important than being nice. Which I wasn't going to evaluate too much. Because right now I needed to make my way to Willa and Gunner. Ivy needed some patience.

If Willa was talking to Gunner, then she must still be the Willa from our past. I wanted her to talk to me.

"Willa." I called out her name just before she walked into the school. She paused and looked back over her shoulder at me. A confused almost startled expression touched her brow. "Hey," I said, unsure what to do now I had her attention.

"Hey," she replied just above a whisper. Was she nervous?

"I saw you rode with Gunner."

She nodded but said nothing more.

"We were all friends once. I do something wrong? You don't seem to like me much."

Her eyes widened; then she shook her head. "No . . . but you've not spoken to me."

She hadn't talked to me. I was letting her make the move to say something. Willa had always been the outgoing one between us. She hadn't let us get away with much, and she was the one to pull me into talking when I didn't want to. Had she changed that much?

"Since when did I have to come after you to talk? The girl I remember used to hunt me down."

A hint of a smile almost lit her lips. Almost. "That was a long time ago."

Yeah, it was, but I was still as attracted to her now as I had been then. She was quieter now and not sure of herself. Almost timid. I didn't imagine Willa turning out this way. Especially looking like she did.

I shifted the one book in my hand to the other arm, then held out my right hand. "Hello, Willa Ames. I'm Brady Higgens. It's nice to meet you."

This time she smiled and slipped her hand into mine as we shook. "You're still crazy," she replied.

I shrugged. "If it ain't broke, don't fix it."

Pursing her lips, she looked adorable. "Hmmm . . . cocky much?"

Actually, no I wasn't. Gunner was cocky. West used to be cocky until he fell in love with Maggie. But me, I was the good guy. I had my life planned out ahead of me. I would be choosing a college soon from the all the offers I'd had for my talent on the football field. But I wasn't cocky. I was determined and driven.

"Just crazy," I told her.

"Friend rule. Good ones don't leave you cornered by those two leeches," Gunner said, interrupting us and drawing Willa's attention from me to him.

She smirked at him. "Maybe I'm not a good friend then."

Gunner smiled at her with a look I knew. He was interested. Dammit. Why did I care? I had my hands full with Ivy. Who was good to me. My main focus was football, and she supported that. Reconnecting with a girl from my childhood because she was gorgeous and there was a past emotional connection didn't justify risking what I already had.

"I'll teach you. I have faith in you, Willa Ames. You'll be my wingman before it's all over," Gunner said.

I liked the wingman comment. That was keeping it real. Gunner didn't do relationships. He just did sex.

Willa chuckled, and the sound felt warm over my skin. "I'm sure I'll be a pro soon."

I couldn't decide if this was as platonic as they sounded or if they were flirting.

"Brady," Ivy called, and my guilt came back. Here I was getting all weird about Gunner and Willa while Ivy was trying to talk to me. What was wrong with me? This was not my typical behavior.

"You're being summoned," Gunner said, looking amused. "We'll catch up with you later. Come on, Wingman, let's go get your books for first period."

Willa gave me a small, tight smile, then turned to walk away with Gunner. Down the hallway.

"Who is that?" Ivy asked. "She new?"

Two things about Lawton: It was fucking small, and everyone knew everything about everyone. So that question didn't even sound believable. Ivy knew exactly who Willa was by this point, and the girls in town were all talking about her. Now that she was seen talking to me and Gunner, people would do their research and remember just who Willa Ames was, and the three of us would start being on the tongues of gossips everywhere.

The Reality of Being Broken

CHAPTER 10

WILLA

I *wasn't* a good friend. They just didn't know how bad of one I was. Yet. Eventually it would get out. My past and the reason I was here in Lawton, living with my grandmother. But for now I could enjoy not being alone.

Gunner had walked with me to my first-period class, chatting on about a party this Saturday night and acting as if I would be there too. No one had invited me to a party. I had no idea who Asa Griffith was, although the name was familiar. I'd heard it being mentioned yesterday more than one time. Even more than the football game on Friday night, and that was talked about a lot. Probably talk of his party.

When Gunner had finally said his good-bye and gone to his own classroom, I was once again left to myself. No one approached me as I made my way to the desk the teacher had directed me to yesterday. My homework was complete and as perfect as I could make it.

Someone took the chair beside me, and I glanced through my lashes to see a tall guy with dark hair, almost black. His shoulders were wide, making him seem more impressive and large. The tan color of his skin made me think of beaches and sunshine and not Lawton, Alabama. He turned to me, and I quickly moved my eyes back to the notebook on my desk.

"You must be Willa Ames," his deep voice said, drawing my attention back to him.

"Yes," I replied, wishing I knew who he was. I searched his face to see if I recognized him. Everyone had changed so much over the past six years I had a hard time remembering them all.

"You don't remember me, do you? But then I was about seven inches shorter and less muscle or no muscle the last time we saw each other."

I forced a smile. I felt awkward not remembering who he was, but then would he have recognized me if he didn't have the knowledge that the new girl was Willa Ames? I wouldn't beat myself up about it. Although I had gone to school with a lot or most of these kids, I'd not run in their social circles. My only friends had been Gunner and Brady. I didn't get invited to birthday parties as a child, or any party for that matter. I was the Lawtons' help's granddaughter, who had been brought into this world by a "slutty" teenage mother.

He grinned and dimples appeared. Not expected on a guy his size. "Asa . . . Griffith," he said, adding his last name as an afterthought. This was the party guy whose name I had heard before. Digging in my memory, I tried to think of a boy's face that might resemble the much more mature one in front of me now. Had he come to play with Gunner often as a child? I couldn't remember all the friends Gunner had over.

He chuckled this time. "Don't guess I made an impression on you back in the day, but then you'd always been Gunner's. We didn't get to see you much when we came over after Nash called you hot once. Gunner got all pissy, and that was the last time we ever played with you."

That struck a memory.

"Y'all have changed with puberty" was the only comment I had to that.

His dimples deepened, clearly flirting at this point. "And so have you."

I wasn't going to try and decipher what he meant by that. I just smiled and turned back to the notebook in front of me.

"You coming to my birthday party Saturday night? I'll be the big one eight."

Was this an invite? I glanced back over at him. "I wasn't aware I was invited."

He continued to grin. "I'm officially inviting you. I just figured Gunner or Brady already had."

Should I agree to this? The last time I partied . . . I didn't want to think about that right now. It was different. Everything about that night had been different. This was a birthday party with football players. I could do this and not feel guilty. Couldn't I?

"That frown concerns me. I'm not a bad guy. Promise," Asa added as I realized he was watching me and I hadn't responded to his invitation. Which was rude.

"I'm sorry. I was just thinking about my schedule. But yes, I'd like to come. Thank you for inviting me." I sounded entirely too formal. Trying not to wince at my own ridiculous response, I once again stared down at my notebook.

"I think I make you nervous, Willa Ames. I like that." He sounded amused, and I didn't look back at him.

"Will Gunner be walking you to your next class like he did this one, or can I have that honor?" He was mimicking my formal tone, and I bit back a smile. I think I liked Asa Griffith.

"I'd like that," I replied, letting the smile touch my

lips. It felt good to want to smile again. I was doing it more and more since my arrival in Lawton. A few months ago I thought I'd never smile again.

But with that thought the reality of what I'd seen, what I'd done, and all I'd lost came back to me. The darkness I carried like bricks on my back weighed me down, and I once again lost my smile.

The teacher began to talk, and I gave him my attention, even if the past was haunting my thoughts and reminding me why I'd never truly be normal again.

Asa attempted to talk to me several times during class, and I managed a smile, if not a response, each time. My chest was heavy, but I wanted to feel normal again, if only for a moment. Was that selfish of me? Should I get to feel normal?

When the bell rang—ending my wasted class, since my mind hadn't registered one thing that the teacher had said—I picked up my books and stood up.

"What class do you have next?" Asa asked as he got up to walk with me toward the door. I guess he was serious about walking me there.

"Lit," I replied.

"I'm two doors down in Spanish. Also, saw you get out of Gunner's truck today. Had any trouble with Kimmie yet?"

I wasn't sure what that meant. Kimmie was the girl from the restroom yesterday and one of the girls who had bombarded Gunner when we'd arrived. I knew that much, but as for me having any issues with her, I hadn't dealt with that. She didn't pay much attention to me.

"No," I replied.

He nodded. "You will. She's not going to be able to handle you at all."

If he meant she would be jealous of me, then she was just silly. Gunner wasn't serious about her or anyone for that matter. Girls who were blind to teenage boys who clearly didn't care about them were sad. They thought the television romance was real. It wasn't. This was not *One Tree Hill*. It was real life.

"He referred to me as his wingman this morning. She doesn't need to worry about me. She needs to worry about all the girls who are stupid enough to think they have a chance at an actual relationship with him. Like her."

Asa laughed loudly. "Damn I like you."

"Thanks." I was going to say more when my eyes met Gunner's as he made his way toward me.

"And here he comes," Asa said, once again sounding amused.

Gunner's eyes went from me to Asa as if he were annoyed. I wasn't sure why he would be, and if he acted annoyed, I was going to set him straight. But that wasn't going to happen right now because Kimmie stepped in front of him, blocking his path. Which made Asa laugh again.

"One day he'll figure out that a quickie from Kimmie means weeks of her up his ass."

"Has he done this with her before?" I asked, watching him move her out of his way with both his hands on her shoulders. His scowl was surprising. I'd never seen him pissed like that before.

"Been happening since ninth grade. She's an easy lay, but then she clings. We've all learned our lesson, but Gunner can't seem to shake her."

I wonder what it was about her that kept drawing him back in.

"Kind of like Ivy and Brady. Except Brady doesn't seem to mind Ivy's clingy ways. He lets it happen because she's hot. I think in Ivy's head they're an item. Brady however doesn't see it as an exclusive thing. But then none of the guys have tried to bang her either."

I had been away from high school drama, dealing with real world stuff, for so long now I found it pointless. Once I'd been that girl wrapped up in a guy, thinking he loved me. Not knowing what was really happening when I wasn't around. Never once guessing the truth until it was right there in front of me. What I thought was a broken heart then didn't even touch the reality of being broken.

"Here's your class," Asa said, stopping my thoughts from going dark once again.

"Thank you."

He shrugged and on his tall frame it looked out of place. Like that of a little boy, not a massive football player. "I'll see you at lunch?" I think it was a question. It sounded like one. So I simply nodded, then walked into the room. Wishing I had a distraction in this period to help me push away the pain.

Like a Vacuum

CHAPTER 11

GUNNER

When I walked into Spanish, Asa was grinning at me like a fucking idiot. I'd seen him with Willa, and he thought walking her to class was one-upping me.

"I invited your girl to my party," he said as I put my books down on the desk beside him.

"Willa isn't my girl." I glared at him. I wasn't playing games with him. I had Kimmie shit to deal with. She was full-force annoying now that Willa had ridden to school with me.

"Good. I was hoping she was available" was his response, also meant to piss me off.

"Stop being an ass."

He cocked one eyebrow. "I'm serious. Completely."

Well, hell. I wasn't ready for that. Willa was back, and she was all grown up. I should have prepared for one of the guys other than Brady to go after her.

"Back off," I warned him. Why? I didn't want to think about that.

He smirked, then shook his head. "Nope."

Fucker.

I ignored Asa most of the period, except when Nash turned around and started talking about Friday night. We had a football game to focus on, which was more important than Saturday night and Asa's birthday party at the field. We would all end up at the field on Friday night after the game, too. In a small town like Lawton, the field was how we spent our weekends. Away from the adults.

Serena kept staring back at me and licking her lips slowly. I guess she was insinuating we hook up, and if we weren't currently in the classroom, I'd let her at it. I needed the tension relief. All this Asa and Willa crap fucking with my head. My choice to take Serena to the homecoming dance was simply on her skill in the blow-job department.

"I think I might sell tickets to the Kimmie and Serena fight. All the hair pulling and screaming will be hot. Think you can get them to set up a time and place so I can make some quick cash?" Nash asked, glancing back at Serena.

"Doubt it. Kimmie will go at her whenever the mood strikes. Serena on the other hand would probably be more accommodating," I replied with a grin.

"Never got why you and West wasted time with Serena. She's been there and done it all," Asa said, unimpressed.

"Heard she's like a vacuum," Nash informed him.

They both looked at me for confirmation. I shrugged. "Her middle name should be Hoover."

Laughter erupted from both of them, and we were all glared at by Mr. Jones. We had interrupted his porn, I would guess. The old, fat Spanish teacher rarely did much teaching. He gave us worksheets and online programs during class. A couple of kids had caught him watching online porn on his MacBook while sitting up there. Shame we couldn't do the same. This class would be a hell of a lot more fun.

"So back to Willa," Asa began, and I rolled my eyes. "Why'd she move back in with her grandmother? Thought her momma settled down and shit and sent for her back then."

I'd wondered the same thing. But the reason why was something Willa wasn't willing to talk about. I'd tried to get her on the subject, and she'd closed up fast. She had secrets that obviously hurt. I got that and I respected it. I had my own damn secrets. Ones that had changed my life. She could keep hers because I sure as hell wasn't sharing mine.

"Not my business or yours."

Asa frowned. "So it's a big deal? Like did she get kicked out or something?"

He was going to push because he was a nosy-ass motherfucker. "I said it ain't our business. Leave it."

Nash turned back around in his chair, and I slammed my book closed just before the bell rang, freeing me from Asa's questioning. Truth was I wanted to know what her secret was. I wanted to know if she'd done something terrible. I couldn't imagine it, but why else would she be back here?

However, it wasn't Asa's business. He didn't know Willa or her past. He hadn't sat with her and held her when she cried because she thought her mother didn't love her. Or the day she found out she was moving away from her nonna. That had been me. Not Brady. Me.

It had been six years and puberty had hit, but we had a history, and I would protect her the best I could. Something lost and hurt in her eyes said she needed protecting. I had made sure to protect the little girl she had once been.

"So you good with me walking her to her next class?" Asa asked me as we headed out the door. I started to come up with some excuse as to why he couldn't when I saw

Brady standing at the door to her classroom and her smiling up at him.

"Never mind. I was beat to it," Asa grumbled, then walked the other way.

I, on the other hand, walked right up to the both of them. We were all friends after all.

"What class do you have next?" I asked her, interrupting whatever Brady had been saying.

They both turned their gazes on me. I could feel Brady's frustration rolling off him in waves. I knew him oh too well. The good boy wasn't thinking of Willa as a friend. He would be the perfect loyal boyfriend that she deserved. I knew it but I didn't like it. I also wasn't that nice of a guy. I wouldn't allow it. Brady was my best friend, and Willa wasn't about to take him away from me with her long legs, bubble butt, and plump lips. Hell no. I wouldn't become the third wheel to the two of them.

West had saddled himself with Maggie like it was the best damn thing in the world. He was nuts. Brady wasn't about to do that. He had a football career to focus on, and I had frat parties and coeds in my future.

Him getting serious with Willa would ruin all of that.

As his best friend, I would protect his best interests, and I would protect Willa, too.

Six Years Doesn't Change That

CHAPTER 12

BRADY

The first chance I got with Willa all day where Ivy wasn't smothering me and Gunner interrupted us. I'd just gotten her to laugh, too. What was his deal? This was going to cause an issue if we didn't talk it out. I would start on the football field later today. By pounding his ass with the ball every chance I got.

"I have Spanish," she said, pointing to the classroom Gunner had just exited. "Right there."

"You won't learn shit in there. Jones watches porn on his MacBook most of the class," Gunner informed her, making her laugh as her eyes widened.

He wasn't lying. The man really did. He'd been caught

before, but somehow he was still teaching in the classroom. I didn't think we should be telling Willa about it though. Kind of seemed disrespectful.

"I've got a book in my purse I can read," she told Gunner.

"Well, that sounds real entertaining." Gunner sounded mocking, and she just smirked at him as if she wasn't surprised by that response.

"Once you read all the Harry Potters with me, and we talked for hours about them."

Gunner nodded. "Yep, then I had sex and it was all over."

Again Willa's eyes flared, and I elbowed Gunner to shut him up. Jesus! She didn't want to talk about his sex life. He had to stop treating her like a dude. When we were kids, it was different. She wanted to do the things we did, but life changed.

"Ignore his crude ass," I finally said, stopping Gunner from any more inappropriate comments.

"Willa can hear the word *sex*. She knows what it is," Gunner drawled, his gaze still on Willa.

Her face flushed, and I wanted to put Gunner on his ass for embarrassing her.

"On that note, I think I'll go to my next class. I have a novel to read, and from the way it sounds, I'm going to get an entire period to read it." Willa smiled at both of us, making very little eye contact, then hurried to her next class.

I glared at Gunner. "You embarrassed her," I snapped.

He just grinned, still watching her retreating form. "I know. It was hilarious. What seventeen-year-old girl blushes over the word *sex*? Now if I'd said *fuck*, then I might have expected that reaction."

I should have gone on and left him, but I couldn't just yet. I was confused by what his motives were with Willa. "She's not a backseat whore. You realize that right?"

He nodded, then finally looked at me. "Yeah. She's our friend. Six years doesn't change that."

She had been his best friend. If I hadn't been so jealous of the fact he got to see her all the time when *I* wanted to see her all the time, I would have cared that she was the best friend and I was the runner up. When she had left, I had moved into that spot with Gunner, but it hadn't felt right. I missed Willa. For years.

I may have never stopped.

"Why is she back?" I asked him. "There has to be a reason."

Gunner shrugged. "That's her secret. If she wants to tell us, she will. Until then, it's her secret to keep."

He sounded almost defensive of her. Like he was telling me to back off. I'd been talked to like this before where

Willa was concerned. When we were kids, he never let me get too close. There was always a protective wall he held around her, and God forbid anyone get too close.

"I'm worried about her. Her eyes are sad and guarded."

Gunner didn't respond immediately. He looked as if his thoughts had gone far away from here. Almost distant. I waited to see if he'd respond, and when I had almost given up on him, he turned to me. "Not everyone's life is like yours. There are some things people don't want to share. It's how they survive."

At that Gunner walked away. He didn't want to hear what I had to say in response, and I was glad because I didn't have anything. For starters, how the hell was my life different from his, except he had a shit ton of money? We both had married parents and good home lives. Neither of us had seen abuse or been neglected. Well, maybe emotionally Gunner had suffered neglect, but it wasn't all bad. Ms. Ames was always there to mother him when he needed it.

After Willa had left, we stayed closed at first. Then we began to drift. I wasn't sure why, but Gunner pulled away from me for a time. Football and field parties eventually brought us closer again, but things had never really been the same since she left. We'd been closer then. He had been my best friend before then. I thought of West as my best friend now. I talked to West about things Gunner just didn't seem interested in.

Having Willa back reminded me of how things once were. She had been such a big part of our childhood. Being around her again brought it all back.

Willa was dealing with real shit. She'd never had it easy. I knew she thought of herself as a burden to her mother. I had seen it in her eyes and the way she said things. The way she tried so hard to make her nonna proud of her. The day she'd told me she was moving to Arkansas to live with her mother I had wanted to be happy for her. But I'd been heartbroken instead.

That hadn't been roses for her there, either. I could see that in the girl she had become. I hated her mother. I'd only seen her once, and even as a child I knew she was beautiful. But that didn't make me hate her less. She had made Willa feel unwanted.

"You waiting on me?" Ivy's voice broke into my thoughts. She was something else I really needed to deal with. I knew it was obvious that I watched Willa. To everyone but Willa. But I didn't want to hurt Ivy, either. Until Willa walked back into town, I had been perfectly happy doing whatever it was me and Ivy were doing. Which, to be honest, we were mostly just fucking. But still. She was a sweet girl.

I couldn't keep doing that though. Not with Willa being on my brain all the time. It wasn't fair to Ivy. I had to work through what this was I felt for Willa, and if friendship was all we would ever have. Until then I needed my freedom to find out.

Gunner wanted nothing more than friendship. He wasn't mentally capable of being what Willa needed or deserved. He was the good-time guy, not the guy to lean on. Even if he was different with Willa.

"I was just talking to Gunner. Heading to my next class," I told her, not wanting to give her false hope.

Her smile fell, but I'd been nice about the truth. "Oh" was her response.

I should have felt bad about that. I just didn't seem to have the energy to feel anything about her at all. Which didn't say a lot about me as a person. I was letting myself down. Typically I was a better guy than this.

Nothing but Disappointment

CHAPTER 13

WILLA

The thickness of hilarity hangs over me, and I move slowly through the room. Poppy's house is always my favorite escape. There is no sense of annoyance from my being here. I'm accepted and free of the pain that always haunts me. Even my stepfather's disgusted glare that I'm met with every day when he returns from work seems funny right now as I think about it and him. The world is my playground, and I shall play in it. I giggle loudly, and Bo, Poppy's boyfriend, looks up at me from his spot on the worn leather sofa and smiles. It's crooked and sweet, like Bo. Poppy is lucky to have Bo. He is sincere, fun, kind—but best of all he never fails to supply the good stuff.

Bo's older brother sells pot, and he makes sure Bo gets the best when we all pitch in and buy some. We can count on him for nights like this. Sometimes days like this. Poppy's parents are rarely home. They both work long hours at the restaurant they own in town, and Poppy has to always stay home and keep an eye on her younger sister. Which is funny too. Not sure why it's funny, but I laugh again.

The room is almost weightless as I float by and then stop to pick up the vodka Sprite that Poppy fixed me. Bo's brother also bought us a bottle of vodka. I drink the sweet mixture, glad that Poppy put so much Sprite in it. I don't like the taste of alcohol much, but it sure makes me feel happy. So happy.

The yellow walls of the kitchen are too bright, so I turn off the lights and begin searching for the cheese balls I saw earlier in the pantry. I love cheese balls and all their fattening goodness. "Where's the cheese balls?" I yell from the corner of the pantry.

"I got 'em," Poppy calls back, so I stumble out of the pantry, only falling on my ass once and laughing so hard I have to curl up in a ball on the split-brick floor. The cold brick feels good to my face, so I rub it around, letting my cheek be soothed.

"Are you making out with the floor?" someone asks, and I open my eyes to see Cole Sanders standing over me

with his glass of straight vodka and an e-cigarette he put the good juice into. He gets away with smoking pot all over the place with that thing. Lucky.

"Maybe." I grin, holding both my hands in the air. "Or maybe I can't get up."

"Maybe I need to come down there and join you," he says, not reaching for my hands, then winks.

I'm high, but I'm not high enough to let Cole Sanders down here with me. He's slept with so many girls he's bound to have an STD by now. No way. I shake my head and sit up quickly. "Not happening," I say just before struggling to stand up.

He acts as if he were pouting. "Ah, Willa, that hurts."

Rolling my eyes, I reach for my drink. "Not as much as the herps you'd give me."

"SLAM!" Bo hollers, laughing hysterically at my comeback. I join him in his laughter and so does Cole.

Life is funny. Everything is just hilarious. I love it here. I love pot and vodka and Bo's brother.

I love—

Then Poppy's screams fill the air, and fear consumes me.

I bolted up in bed and placed my hand on my heart, trying to catch my breath. The screaming was still there. In my head. It would always be there. I'd never forget it as long as I lived. Tears slid down my face, and I buried my head in my hands as the pain that came with this nightmare returned. I hated remembering, yet I had to. It was only fair that I did.

Forgetting meant living, and was that even fair? No. Nothing was fair. It never would be again. Just like nothing would ever be normal. Especially me. I was broken in ways that could never be fixed. My life would always have the shadow of pain, guilt, regret, and loss.

Dropping my hands, I swung my legs over the bed and stood up. I had to see her. Remember her and allow the searing heartache to run its course. There would be no more sleep tonight. I was afraid to close my eyes now. I didn't want to see the rest. I lived it. I tried like hell to block it and unsee it, but I couldn't. It was there in my mind, burned deeply into me. As it should be.

I opened the dresser drawer and moved the photo albums I had there over until I found the one picture I had kept. The others I'd left behind. I was sure my mother had thrown them out by now. I didn't want them anyway. Too many memories. This was all I could stand. Seeing this one.

Flipping it over, I saw Poppy's strawberry-blond hair first. It was teased sky high, and she was laughing at me. My hair was equally ridiculous. The bright colors we wore went beyond hideous, but the pink lipstick and blue eye shadow were the best parts. It was homecoming week last year, and this had been our outfit for Eighties Day. Our mothers had grown up in the eighties, so they'd both been very helpful with the wardrobes. We had nailed the look.

As awesome as we were dressed up, that wasn't why I had chosen this photo. It was the laughter on Poppy's face, on both our faces. It was what I remembered most about Poppy. The laughing and the feeling like I had someone who cared. When I had left Lawton at eleven, I'd thought I would never have a friend again.

Then Poppy had shared her peanut butter sandwich with me because my mother had forgotten to make me a lunch. It had been instant friendship.

My chest clinched tightly until it was only pain. Tears blurred my vision, and I slipped the photo back in the drawer and covered it with the albums. That was a life I'd never have again. Laughter I'd never feel. Even now when I smiled, I felt guilty for being able to. I didn't deserve to smile and definitely not laugh. Ever again.

I often wished I was physically unable to laugh and smile. It felt good when I did, until I remembered why I shouldn't. The guilt was consuming. It ate at me. It destroyed me.

Looking around the dark room, I wondered what life would have been like had my mother never sent for me. If

I'd stayed here in Lawton. Lived this life instead. Gunner and Brady both seemed okay. They weren't unstable. It was safe in this small town. But hadn't it been safe in the one I'd lived in too?

Bad decisions could have been made anywhere. Like me. I was a product of my mother's bad decision. She'd made that in this small town, and I'd been nothing but disappointment.

I'll Collect When the Time Is Right

CHAPTER 14

GUNNER

I stopped by my father's office door on my way downstairs for breakfast. It was closed as always. When I was five, I had wanted to show him a turtle I had found and went barging in that door unannounced and invited. He'd been on the phone while I'd been jumping back and forth on my feet with the thrilling news of my new pet. Trying hard to keep quiet until he was off the phone so I could show him. Ms. Ames had been happy when I had shown her, so I thought maybe I could make my father equally happy.

It was something I did often back then. Try to please the man. Make him smile at me. The eternity of his phone conversation had been enough of a reason to praise me, because I was rarely quiet. When he had ended the call, he'd leveled his dark brown eyes, very different from my own, on me and glared with fury.

"Why are you in here, Gunner?"

I held out my turtle, who I had named Charlie Daniels because Ms. Ames listened to music by that name often and I liked to dance to it in the kitchen. "I found a turtle!" I announced with great pride.

My father looked down at the turtle and then back at me. The rule was I wasn't supposed to go in his office. He didn't like me in here the way he did Rhett. Sometimes I wondered if he even liked me at all. But I'd found a turtle, and he needed to see it.

"If you ever walk in that door again without being invited in, I will take off this belt and beat your ass. Do you understand me?" His voice was a little less than a roar. I didn't understand him at all. He'd not even acknowledged my turtle. So I held it up higher. Until my elbows were over my head. "But I found a turtle!" I exclaimed, thinking he had somehow missed this information.

My father reached in my hand and took the turtle from it, then tossed it out the open window behind his desk. "There. Go find the damn thing and stay out of my office."

I never did find my turtle.

And I never called him Dad or Father again.

The man behind that door I hated. I knew he hated me equally, and it wasn't until much later that I had understood his hate. One day I'd demand my mother tell me my real father's name. I wanted to carry that last name. I no longer cared about the name that held power in this small southern town. I wouldn't live here much longer. When I graduated, I'd take my money and leave. Never to return.

Except maybe to throw a party the day of that man's funeral.

The kitchen already smelled like muffins, bacon, and coffee when I entered it. My parents never came to the kitchen to get food. They would sit at the table in the dining room, and Ms. Ames would serve them their meal. I, however, had started eating in here with Willa when we were kids. I liked it better at the small, round table that was always set whenever I walked in.

"Morning, boy," Ms. Ames said with real affection in her voice. "'Bout time you got down here. You're gonna be late. I put your coffee in a travel mug, and here's your two blueberry muffins and a few slices of bacon. Don't eat and drive. Just eat it quick before you go."

I was in a bigger hurry than she realized. I had to get Willa and get us both to school on time. "I'll eat in first period," I told her, taking the food and coffee from her hands.

She frowned but nodded. "Okay then. You drive safe."

"Will do," I assured her.

My mother wouldn't wake for another two hours. It was a blessing. Having to face her before I'd had coffee every morning would suck. I never saw the man in the office, and I liked to keep it that way. One of the reasons I never showed for family meals. I told Mom that dinner in the kitchen was easier on my schedule for football and homework. It was complete bullshit, but for the most part it worked.

"Willa doing okay at school? You seen her?"

"She's doing just fine from what I've seen, but I'll watch out for her," I replied, then hurried out the door. I wanted time with Willa, and the more I wasted in the house chatting up her nonna the less I'd have on my ride to school with her.

She made me remember a happier time. A simple, easy friendship I no longer knew. I wanted it back. Being with her hadn't just been easy, it had made me feel good. It still did. My chest felt lighter, and I looked forward to being around her. No one calmed me and excited me at the same time the way Willa did.

I took a long swig of my coffee and let it burn my throat on the way down before starting my truck and making my way to Ms. Ames's house the long way in case anyone was watching.

Willa was outside at the end of her driveway, with the brown backpack she carried on one shoulder and a bottle of water in her other hand. Her blond hair was dancing in the breeze as the early morning sun illuminated her. She really was gorgeous. It sucked that I needed her friendship too much to ruin it by getting to put my hands on her.

I stopped beside her and watched as she climbed inside and looked at my uneaten muffin and three slices of bacon on the napkin on my seat. Her hand reached out, and she snatched a slice, then took a bite before smiling at me. "Next time get her to give you more. She expects me to eat cereal since she leaves so early."

I'd keep that in mind. "You can have the muffin. I've already eaten one of them. But leave me the rest of the bacon."

She took a muffin and began eating like she was starving. I wasn't sure a girl had ever eaten like that in front of me. Most didn't eat in front of me at all, or in front of any guys for that matter.

"Ms. Ames starving you this week?" I asked, amused.

She nodded, then smiled. "I have a high metabolism, and I require food."

"Someone needs to tell your nonna then. She should be sending you off with more than cereal for breakfast."

She shrugged. "Why would I do that if I have you to

smuggle it out to me from the big house? Y'all get the good stuff."

I knew she meant the more expensive meals. My mother required uppity healthy shit that cost money and was bought at that organic grocery in Franklin. "Fine. I'll keep you fed. But you owe me. I'll collect when the time is right."

She laughed, and although it didn't fully touch her eyes, it was definitely a laugh. Something I wanted to hear more of. Willa had a really good laugh.

I Don't Drink Alcohol

CHAPTER 15

BRADY

Taking Ivy to Asa's birthday party didn't help how she viewed our relationship. It also didn't give me the opportunity to spend time with Willa. Who had shown up with Gunner. Not that they had stayed together. Gunner had taken off to the woods with Serena a few minutes ago, and Willa was currently talking to Maggie and West. Maggie appeared to like Willa, as did the birthday boy, who kept moving toward her wherever she went. Damn horny-ass Asa.

Maybe I could get Maggie to invite Willa over so I could have time alone with her that Gunner couldn't interrupt. He said he wanted friendship. I didn't believe him, but I think he *thought* that was all he wanted. He just didn't realize yet he wanted Willa like I did. I was just ready to face it. I was interested in getting to know the girl she'd become. When we were kids, I'd had a crush on her simply because she was different. Most girls I knew wouldn't get dirty playing ball or go looking for lizards. She'd been fascinating to me as a kid. Now that she was all grown up, she was still different but beautiful. Willa was like this untouched flower that everyone wanted to see and get close to.

"I want another beer," Ivy said as she looped her arm through mine and held on to me like she needed me in order to stand up. She had drunk two Dixie cups full of the beer that we had sitting in a keg on the back of Nash's truck. She was maybe 110 pounds soaking wet. She didn't need another cup of beer. Soon she'd be vomiting on my feet and gross shit like that. I wasn't taking her home trashed.

"You've had plenty. Grab a bottle of water out of the cooler. Or a diet soda or something." Anything but more beer.

She pouted, and her lips stuck out in an annoying way. I never really liked the pouty-lip thing. It was meant to manipulate, and that got on my nerves. I didn't want to be manipulated. "You'll puke, then pass out, and I'll be left to explain all that to your parents when I take you home."

Sighing dramatically, she glanced over at Ginger, one of

the girls on the cheerleading squad, who was snuggled up to Ryker Lee. Ginger had been after him for weeks. He'd finally given her a notice tonight.

"He's no fun," she whined. "Come on, Ginger. Let's go dance!" she exclaimed, already too tipsy.

Ginger wiggled her body against Ryker. "Want to dance with me?"

He winked at her and nodded his head in the direction of the music someone had blaring on their Beats Pill. "Go on, and I'll watch."

Ginger beamed at him, excited about being able to show off. "M'kay," she replied, and sauntered off, swaying her hips like she knew she was being watched.

"Dayum girl's begging for it," Ryker drawled.

I chuckled. "Seems that way."

Ryker shook his head, then turned his attention toward Willa, who was now standing up from the log she'd been sitting on while talking to West and Maggie. She looked like she might be about to go somewhere. As much as I'd like to make sure she didn't want Gunner, I also didn't want her going looking for him and seeing him and Serena going at it.

"You enjoy your view," I told him. "I'm gonna go check on something."

Ryker laughed. "Sure you are. I'd check on that too."

I didn't respond or look back at him. He knew where I was headed, and he also didn't blame me. I could see it in his eyes when he looked Willa's way. She was beautiful, but there were several beautiful girls in Lawton. It was the fact she was new. They all were attracted to the newness of her. A girl they hadn't made out with or wanted to since they were in junior high.

Willa was a fantasy they hadn't worn out yet. She also had an air of mystery around her that appealed to guys. We wanted to get past her barriers. See her smile. Gunner could never be the guy she needed. Willa seemed fragile now. Gunner was terrible with fragile. He'd break her too easily. I could keep her safe and make her smile again.

Willa was walking away from my cousin and West when I walked up to her. She had made her getaway and was headed for the woods behind the clearing. Through the woods was where all the cars were parked. Which meant that was where she would find Gunner's truck and Gunner in a probably compromising situation.

"Willa," I called out, and she stopped, then turned around.

She was dressed warm for the chilly late-fall evening, unlike the other girls here, wearing jeans and a dark blue hoodie. Willa hadn't come to draw attention to herself. "Hey," she replied with a small smile.

"You leaving?" I asked, hoping that wasn't what she

wanted to do, because her ride was definitely busy.

"Uh, well, it's late, and I'm tired. I saw Gunner head back here earlier, and I was hoping I could find him and see if he'd mind giving me a ride back to Nonna's."

Uh, yeah. Bad idea.

"I could use some company. It'll be hard to find him out there, and he did take Serena with him. Might not want to walk up on that," I said with an apologetic smile.

Her eyes widened like she hadn't thought of that.

"Oh, yeah. No I don't."

I could take her home, but that would mean leaving Ivy to get hammered on her own. I'd picked her up at her house, and her dad had met me at the door. Made me promise to take care of her and have her home on time. I couldn't bring her home drunk and past her curfew. So leaving to take Willa home wouldn't be possible.

"Want a drink?" I asked her.

She shook her head. "I don't drink."

"You don't drink? Why haven't you died from dehydration yet?" I was teasing her.

She rolled her eyes. "I don't drink alcohol."

"I wasn't offering you a beer. We have water and sodas too."

Her eyes lit up. "In that case, yes. My mouth is dry. I'd love a water."

"Come this way," I said, being sure to walk behind the crowd of people with Willa so Ivy wouldn't spot me and swoop in to stake the claim she did not have on me.

We walked around the trucks that did park in the clearing of the field. We needed lights, somewhere to keep the keg, and extra seating, so a few drove their trucks right up in here. Ivy was dancing with Ginger and doing her best to entertain whoever was around. The Dixie cup in her hand made me mutter a curse. She'd be drunk and stupid the next time we spoke. Ivy had been comfortable and easy, so I'd let our relationship grow into something I never really wanted. I didn't want to hurt her, and honestly, she had started feeling like an obligation. It wasn't fair to her. Or me.

What Does Casual Mean?

CHAPTER 16

WILLA

The cold water felt good as I drank several long gulps before stopping. My mouth had been terribly dry, but I'd thought the only drink they had here came out of that large keg on the back of an old blue pickup truck with really big wheels. I really wanted to be at home in my room, reading in my sweatpants and cozy pink socks with the hearts on them that I'd gotten for Valentine's Day from Poppy last year. The thought of Poppy as always hurt, and I mentally winced.

Seeing everyone so drunk and carefree had taken me back to a time when I was much like them. Except, unlike here, we had added drugs to the mix. There were no worries, and we owned the world. It was a foolish thing to think that way. Like you were invincible. Because no one was. Death would come sooner for some than others.

"Water taste that bad?" Brady asked, and I realized I'd zoned into the dark place I lived often. The one that had been my shield through the months following that night.

"No, it's great. I was just thinking of things I'd rather not."

That was the only truth he would get.

"Come on." He nodded toward the woods. "Let's get out of the noise and enjoy our water. You can tell me about the last six years of your life, and I'll bore you with details of mine."

"No, thanks," was my quick reply. Talking about the darkness wasn't happening. Not even with the counselor they'd made me see in the correctional facility I'd lived in.

He frowned. "You wanted to escape the party."

I smiled because I didn't realize I had sounded completely rude. "I do. I just don't want to talk about my past. It's . . . boring," I lied. Nothing was boring. It was tragic.

"Fair enough. We'll go drink our water and talk about my life. I love to be the center of attention."

That made me laugh. "Okay." Brady put me at ease. Once he had made me feel nervous, silly, and giddy. Now, though, getting to know the older, more mature Brady, I liked him. He was a good guy. Solid. Dependable.

We walked into the woods and toward the vehicles parked on the other side. I noticed the truck I'd seen Brady driving to school. He was apparently taking us there. The moonlight wasn't very bright tonight, but it did illuminate the area some.

"My truck's there. We can go sit on the tailgate," he said, nodding his head in that direction.

"What about your date?" I asked him, remembering the girl I saw him at school with a lot and that he'd arrived with.

He glanced back toward the clearing. "She's drunk and dancing. Won't know I'm missing."

"Oh," I said, wondering about her. I hadn't asked questions at school, but I'd overheard enough to know they were an item. "How long have y'all been dating?" I asked, wanting to get the subject on him immediately, far away from me.

He pulled his tailgate down and motioned for me to hop up. I did, and he sat down beside me. "Not sure exactly. It's been a casual thing for a few months."

Casual? "What does *casual* mean?"

He gave me a crooked grin. "Do y'all not do casual in Arkansas?"

We did, I guess, but what I had seen at school wasn't what I thought of when I thought of casual. "I'm thinking we have two different ideas on what casual is."

"No. We have the same idea. It's Ivy who is confused on the casual thing. She likes to make it more serious than it is." The guilt that flashed in his eyes wasn't hard to miss. He couldn't hide that. I wondered if he even believed what he'd just said.

I was expecting Ivy to come after us at any minute. Hopefully not swinging fists. I wasn't drunk, and it wouldn't be fair to her. After six months living in a facility with tough-ass chicks, I could hold my own. One ass kicking and I'd gotten smart. Made the right friends and learned how to fight. It was the only way to survive that world.

"Have you explained casual to her?" I asked, taking a sip of water. I wanted to know if he'd actually tried to tell Ivy they were casual. Brady was a good guy. But this seemed to tarnish him some. Stringing Ivy along wasn't exactly part of his persona.

He chuckled and shook his head. "No point. She won't listen."

"Then you must really like her."

"Why do you say that?" He frowned like my comment made no sense.

I thought it made complete sense. But then most teenage boys were idiots when it came to females and relationships. At least, that's been my experience.

"Because you continue to keep her around. She can't annoy you too bad."

He was silent a moment, then sighed. "Actually, she annoys the shit out of me. I'm just too nice to hurt her."

He clearly looked torn up about it, but that was a weak response. No girl in her right mind wanted to be pitied and kept because the guy didn't like hurting people's feelings. "If you don't like her, stringing her along isn't exactly nice either."

Brady turned to look at me, and I met his steady blue gaze. I'd always had a thing for his eyes. They were piercing. Once I imagined them looking at me with love, but that had been the fantasy of an eleven-year-old girl who didn't realize what love was exactly. Or what love could do.

"She's got a bad home life. Stepmom is mean to her. Constantly stays on her about her body and appearance. She's insecure."

So? This still didn't mean he had to keep her around if he didn't like her. "If you like her, then own up to it. If you don't, let her go so she can feel free to find someone who does."

He again went silent for a few moments. I drank my water and looked up at the stars visible in the night sky. It was peaceful out here away from the party. I could forget my past and focus on the fact I'm alive. Even if it wasn't fair and I didn't deserve it. I was here. Breathing and able to see the moon as it lit the night sky. These were things I once didn't think about or appreciate. I was too busy trying to find happiness in ways that only lead to bad things. Terrible things.

"You're right," he finally said. I took my gaze from the moon and gave him my full attention.

"Of course I am. I'm a girl. She's a girl. I know how we should be treated. What we deserve. And what you deserve. Life is short. We don't know what will happen tomorrow—as cliché as it sounds, it's very true. I know." I paused before I said more. I didn't want to tell him the hard truths that proved I was right.

He moved so quickly I didn't have time to register what was happening until the warmth of his lips covered mine and his hand slipped into my hair. Then I was fully aware.

Curiosity won the very mini brief conflict in my head. Brady was a friend, and I wasn't anyone that someone could have a relationship with. I was damaged beyond repair. But I wanted to taste this. To give the little girl who had thought she loved Brady Higgens a glimpse at what it was like to be touched by him. Then the little girl could move on from that and live her life. My fantasy complete.

His lips were soft but firm as they moved over mine. His fingers tangled in my hair like they wanted to be there.

As if they had thought of this moment, and now they would relish it.

I sank into him, craving his warmth and the feel of his skin on mine. Inhaling his scent. The cologne he wore was subtle but attractive. I was sure many girls had clung to him just to get near it. It wasn't until his tongue slipped past my lips and into the heat of my mouth that I understood the repercussions of what I was allowing.

Brady was here with another girl. He was my friend and could only ever be my friend because I could never be anything more to anyone. I had demons that haunted me and would my entire life. I had a family I wanted to win forgiveness from, and Nonna had said Brady was off limits. She was all I had left, and I couldn't lose her, too.

Placing both hands on his hard chest, I felt the ache of loss before I pushed away from him. My lips were instantly chilled by the evening air, and I wanted to touch them to hold the warmth there. But I didn't. This was all the fantasy I could get from Brady Higgens.

I stood up, and without a backward glance, I ran.

Where's Willa?

CHAPTER 17

GUNNER

Willa was not here. I'd been gone back to the woods with Serena for about thirty minutes.

Now I was back, however, I couldn't find Willa. Dammit.

"She left with Brady. Went into the woods," Asa said, walking up to me. He sounded as annoyed as I felt.

I started to ask which direction when I spotted Brady coming out of the woods. Alone.

Not waiting for more information from Asa, I went to meet Brady before he got back into Ivy's view and she sidled up to him again.

He held a bottle of water in his right hand, so at least he hadn't been drinking with her. Didn't help the fact he was back and she wasn't. He'd better not have left her in the woods.

"Where's Willa?" I asked with an angry bite in my voice.

Brady turned his eyes to me, and I could see concern there. That calmed my anger down real fast and replaced it with my own worry.

"She okay? Where is she?" I repeated, my voice verging on frantic.

He shrugged and looked back to the woods. "She left. I tried to follow her but lost her. I was hoping she was back here."

He lost her? What the fuck!

"How the hell did you lose her? Was she fucking running?"

Brady didn't respond, and my anger was back. Had she been running? From him? I stepped up until I was in his face. "What did you do?" I demanded as my hands balled into fists at my side.

"We had a conversation. She disagreed with me. Then she took off."

He was lying. His stupid ass made a move on her. I could see it all over his face. "Liar. You fucking kissed her or tried to."

He didn't respond, and I knew I'd guessed right.

"Where'veyoubeen?" Ivy ran her words all together, slurring, and now clinging to Brady's arm to hold her up.

I didn't have time for her shit either. "Which way did she run?" I demanded.

He looked back at the woods. "She ran to the left from where I'm parked. I hoped she'd come back this way. I followed her trail. But she must have turned and headed for the main road instead."

Motherfucker!

I took off running in that direction instead of bashing Brady's face in. He was so damn calm about her being out there in the dark alone. What was he thinking?

"I've got to get Ivy home," he called out after me as if that was an explanation as to why he had let Willa run off alone. I didn't reply.

I just went after Willa. If she was on the road, I'd find her faster in my truck. Heading toward it, I kept my eyes open for her anywhere in the darkness of the parked vehicles, but there was nothing.

This Place Will Turn on You without Question

CHAPTER 18

WILLA

The red Mustang was fairly new, and the girl with long dark hair driving it seemed safe enough. At least I wasn't going to have to walk the seven miles or so back to Nonna's. Although I'd been ready to when the girl pulled up and asked me what I was doing walking in the dark on the deserted road.

I'd told her that my ride was otherwise occupied at the field party. She'd asked me who my ride was, and when I said Gunner Lawton, she rolled her eyes, muttered, "Figures," and offered to give me a lift to my house. She was about my age, but I hadn't seen her at school.

"Thanks," I said as she pulled back onto the road after I got in.

"No problem. It's not exactly safe to be walking out at night. Where do you live?"

"You know Gunner?" I asked.

She made a grimace and nodded.

"Do you know where his house is?"

She glanced at me before looking back at the road. "Everyone knows where the Lawton mansion is."

"I live in the cottage to the back west corner."

She looked at me again. "You live in Ms. Ames's house?"

So she was from around here. I wondered if she went to my school and I'd somehow missed her. "That's my grandmother."

A grin broke across her face. "Willa Ames has returned to Lawton."

And she knew my name.

"You know who I am?" It was a valid question, but I was still surprised.

She laughed. "I just moved back to town too. Although I've only been gone two years. I was here back then, when you, Gunner, and Brady were always together. Every girl in school wanted to be you. Two best friends like that. I was envious of you just like the rest of them. Even if we were just kids."

None of the other girls remembered me. I was surprised this one did. "I didn't realize that." I paused, then glanced back at her. "Thanks for the ride . . ." I left it hanging. Hoping she'd supply me with her name. It almost felt rude to ask.

She grinned, and I felt comfortable with her. It was a smile that wasn't fake but wasn't complete, either. Much like my own.

"Riley Young," she finally said. "The town's most hated citizen."

Hated? That was odd. She was my age and looked nice enough. "Why are you hated?" I asked her, wondering again why I hadn't seen her at school if we'd gone to school together when we were younger.

"No one wants the truth when it doesn't suit. They prefer to weave lies and live in them. It's the way of this place. God knows why I came back."

That wasn't an answer. But it was true. I knew all about truths and the way they hurt too much. Lies made it easier on the living. So I'd suffered the lies told in order to cover the painful reality.

"It's not just that way in this town. It's that way in life," I replied.

She swung her gaze back to me almost as if she was studying me. Surprised by my response. I wondered how many she'd said those same words to who disagreed or didn't understand.

"What brought you back, Willa Ames?" she said, adding my full name as if I were famous.

"Lies that covered the truth," I simply stated.

"That's a bitch, isn't it?"

I nodded. Because it was a bitch. A painful, life-altering bitch.

"Gunner gonna go looking for you and worry over where you are?" Riley asked.

I wasn't sure. Possibly, and I felt guilty for that. Although I'd seen him drink a beer, and I wasn't comfortable riding with someone who had been drinking. I was still on probation. I couldn't mess up. That would definitely be messing up.

"I don't think so," I said, hoping Brady had told him I'd left.

Brady. My face felt hot as I thought about the kiss. I hadn't been able to face him after that. I never wanted to face him again. I'd rather hide in my room and read and block out what I'd done or allowed myself to do.

"Damn. I wanted the asshole to have something to worry about," she said, sounding like she meant it. Apparently she wasn't a fan of Gunner. I wondered if she was one of his many past females.

"I take it you know him well." I was being curious.

She smirked, then shrugged. "Well enough. Better than

I'd like. My life would be easier if I'd never had to return to this town."

Her tone was sad, and I wondered what had happened here. She was my ride home, though, not my new best friend. I wouldn't push for more than she wanted to give me. I stayed silent, and we rode the short distance left to my nonna's.

When her car pulled to a stop outside, I thanked her and got out. Just before I walked inside, I heard her call my name. Stopping, I glanced back at her.

"Be careful who you choose to trust. This place will turn on you without question." Then she gave me a small smile that didn't meet her eyes before rolling back up her window and driving away.

She had been hurt here. That much was obvious.

CHAPTER 19

GUNNER

My hand tightened on the steering wheel as the red Mustang pulled out of the entrance to our estate. She wasn't welcome here. The restraining order against her was enough for me to call the police. Why was she back? No one wanted her here.

With a jerk of my wheel, I cut her escape off and slammed on my brakes. I didn't think it through. I was angry. Seeing her here as if she had the right to drive on my land infuriated me. The lying bitch needed to take her ass back to wherever she ran off to. Lawton didn't want her here.

"Who the fuck do you think you are!" I roared as I stalked

toward her car. The shiny red Mustang her mother had bought her to help ease the fact she'd lied about my brother.

She stared at me as if she were bored and rolled down her window. The urge to bash her headlights with a baseball bat was strong.

"I'm the girl who picked up a very lost, vulnerable Willa Ames walking home in the dark and got her to her grandmother's safely. Not surprising her ride fucked that up." She then backed up her car and drove around my truck without waiting on a response to her news.

I didn't like the idea that Willa had been in her car listening to her lies. However, I was a little relieved that Willa was safely home. Brady and I had both fucked that up. I wasn't sure just yet what the hell had happened back at the field. But I was going to find out.

"Go home," I yelled at the red Mustang.

Riley held her arm out the window and shot me a bird. Classy.

I wanted to talk to Willa tonight, but I didn't have her cell number and I couldn't call Ms. Ames's historic landline. I'd have to wait until tomorrow. At least I knew she was safely inside. I just didn't like thinking about what crazy Riley Young could have possibly said to her.

Riley was the biggest mistake of my life. God I wish she'd stayed gone.

I climbed back in my truck, picked up my phone, and dialed Brady. He'd been looking for Willa too.

"You find her?" he answered, sounding as panicked as I had felt.

"Yeah, she's home," I snapped, still annoyed he'd lost her.

"How'd she get there?"

"She got a motherfucking ride."

He paused. I guess he was waiting on me to tell him who gave her one, but he was going to have to ask if he wanted to know.

"Who?" His question was almost cautious. Like he expected this to be unpleasant.

"Riley," I spat out as if the word alone made me sick.

"Fuck," he muttered.

"Yeah."

"Riley say anything to her?"

"I wouldn't know. Wasn't Willa I talked to. It was Riley. I cut her off as she was leaving the property."

Another muttered curse from Brady.

We sat there in silence for a few moments. Riley had almost ruined my brother's life. What she'd done was unforgivable. Evil. Vindictive.

"You gonna talk to Willa tonight?" Brady finally asked.

"How you expect me to do that? Go knock on the damn door and explain this shit to Ms. Ames?"

"Good point."

Hell yeah it was a good point.

"I'll let you know what she says after I talk to her tomorrow."

He paused, then: "Okay."

Ending the call, I tossed the phone in the cup holder, then headed to the house. A place I hated as much as I hated Riley Young.

She Was a Lot Like You

CHAPTER 20

WILLA

One would expect the wood to be more rotten after years of nonuse. But with paid workers to keep up the Lawton property, the old tree house was in good condition, with no overgrown weeds to crawl over in order to climb the steps. The area looked freshly tended to. That made it even more sad to me.

If the tree house had been forgotten and falling apart from the wear and tear of the weather, I'd have understood its emptiness. It would have been sad too, of course, but not as sad. The lonely tree house, ready for children to play in and build dreams, was empty. Like a beautiful rosebush no one saw or noticed.

I slipped my book into the front of my shorts, because it was too big to fit in my pocket, and climbed the well cared for steps toward the clubhouse where I'd first met my childhood best friends. The familiar smell of the old live oak that housed the Lawton boys' tree house met my nose, and I paused for a moment to inhale. A safer time in my life. One where dark memories didn't haunt me. That was what this represented now. The easy friendships we had had back then were gone now. We'd lost those along with our innocence of youth. Being here reminded me of what I'd been taken away from and how painful that had been.

I climbed the rest of the way and walked into the cabin, complete with a roof that was cone shaped and once reminded me of a castle. Or the tower a princess was locked inside. Pulling out my book, I set it on the wooden bench that was still there. The bean bags were gone now. I was sure they didn't weather well with time. All that was left inside was either made of wood or metal. No toys in boxes or jars with frogs we'd caught lined the shelves.

Turning slowly, I took it all in. This was a time in my life I cherished. It made me happy. Now this place was empty and incomplete without laughter. I sat down on the bench and picked up my book.

"I missed you," I whispered to the walls surrounding me. "It's good to be back."

It sounded silly to be talking to a wooden structure, but it felt right. Like those pieces of lumber understood and recognized me. I liked the idea of that. Besides, I was alone and could sound as ridiculous as I wanted to.

The worn book in my hands smelled of old paper and libraries. I loved that smell. It had gotten me through the past six months. The only escape I had had was inside pages much like these. Pulling my legs up underneath me, I began to read the words and allow the fiction to lead me into another place. One with problems that weren't mine but made me less alone just the same.

I had a chance to find me again. To heal and restore my nonna's trust in me. If I kept my head down, and preferably in a book, I could do just that. Wanting more kisses from Brady Higgens wasn't a step in the right direction. I didn't have time for that. I needed to focus on fixing me.

I got lost within the words, time ticked by, and my brain closed out my surroundings. That was the way it always worked when I read a book. It was because of this that I didn't hear the noise of someone climbing the ladder to join me.

I jumped at the sound of Gunner's voice when he said, "How did I know this was where you'd be?"

Last night I had left without an explanation, and he deserved one. But could I give him an honest one, or was I to pretend it was something else? I wasn't sure if Brady had been honest with him, or if he'd told him a lie in order to protect the truth. I didn't want to lie to Gunner, but the truth was embarrassing too. It could make things weird between us, and I was already dealing with the fact Brady and I would never be the same. There would be no rekindling of friendships with him. Weirdness would become awkwardness that kept a wall between the two of us.

Gunner was bound to notice that eventually.

"Hey" was the best response I could come up with. It sounded weak and wasn't a fair one.

He didn't hit me with the pressure to tell him why I ran. Instead he came inside and sat down on a metal stool across from me, then began to look around the house much the same way that I had. I wondered how long it had been since he'd been here. Were his memories bittersweet like mine?

"God, it still looks the same," he muttered. "Even smells the same."

I nodded. "Except for the lack of sweaty little boys and dirty socks, yes, it does."

Gunner grinned and cut his eyes toward me. "You saying your socks didn't stink?"

"That's exactly what I'm saying," I replied with a smirk.

He chuckled, then turned his attention to the book in

my lap. "You been here to read before, or is this your first time back?"

Again he wasn't demanding an explanation, and that made me feel guilty, because he deserved one. I was sure he had been worried when I had disappeared. He wasn't heartless, and he was my friend. I felt safe telling him the truth. It was a part of who we were. When I needed to talk to someone, Gunner had always been there to listen.

"This is my first time," I answered, wanting to say more.

"It's been about five years for me. Last time I was up here, I brought . . . a girl, and we made out. It was my first time touching tits."

I made a face, and he laughed at me. "What? I'm a guy."

I was well aware he was a guy. "Poor tree house didn't know what was happening. It went from a place to entertain children to a brothel overnight." I was teasing, of course.

Gunner burst into laughter, and I enjoyed the sound. It fit up here. We'd laughed a lot in this house. It was our place to be free of adults.

"It's been maintained well. I expected rotten steps and weeds."

Gunner shrugged. "It's part of the property. They can't let anything look bad on the estate. Plus, this was Rhett's sixth birthday present. Gotta protect that."

The bitterness at the mention of his older brother surprised me. All I had known was a boy who had adored his older brother. What had happened to change that? "Do you and Rhett not get along now?" I asked gently, not wanting to pry too much.

He shrugged. "Nah, we get along fine. He only makes it home about once a year for the holidays, but we talk on the phone some."

That didn't explain his bitter tone when he'd spoken about his brother. "Oh," I said by way of response because I didn't want to push. It wasn't my business.

"He's the favorite, is all. You know that. Didn't change. Never will."

That much I knew. Rhett was definitely the most loved child. His parents were very proud of him, even when we had all been younger. There was nothing that Rhett could do that was frowned upon. They saved all that for Gunner. Not that it was fair at all, but that was how things in this house worked. More times than not, Nonna would leave with a plate of cookies to sneak into Gunner's bedroom because he had gotten in trouble again with his parents over something Nonna didn't agree with.

Even knowing all that, I also knew that something else was there. Under the surface. Something he was hiding and letting simmer and burn beneath his skin. That wasn't going to end well. One day he'd explode and end up with too many regrets to count. I decided to push just a little. The best way to do that was to be slightly vulnerable and see if he opened up. Not because I was nosy, but because I was concerned for the boy who had once been there for me when I needed him most.

"When I left here, I thought I'd be alone forever. No friends again. I was terrified of school in a new place. But then I found Poppy, or she found me. She never left my side. She was a lot like you."

Gunner had gone still, as he seemed truly interested in what I was telling him. Saying Poppy's name wasn't easy. He'd never know how much verbalizing that piece of my past had cost me. My chest was aching, and the thick heaviness of grief began to seep through me. I rarely let myself think of her. Much less say her name aloud. But I wanted others to know her.

She deserved to be remembered. To be shared. Even though her life had been short and the plans we'd made to go off to college together and marry best friends so we could live next door to each other would never happen, her memory was precious. I wanted to say her name even if it pained me to do so.

"You miss her?"

"More than any words could describe."

He raised his eyebrows. "So they made you leave. You didn't want to come back. You had friends and a good life there?"

Those were questions I wouldn't answer. Instead I gave him all I was willing to give him. "Yes and no. My life there is gone now. I don't want to go back. I don't think I can."

"But . . ." He paused, frowning. "What about Poppy?"

I was expecting that question. When I said her name, I'd come to terms with telling him the truth about her. Hearing him say her name hadn't pained me. I was okay with it. She was a part of me now too. I wanted to share her with Gunner. I'd not wanted that before.

"She's dead." Those were words I had refused to say for a very long time. They had gotten stuck in my throat, and the sobbing would begin when I even tried.

"Oh God," he whispered. "How?"

This was the part I hated to say. The part that I wished to God I never had to tell. It was why I was destroyed. Why my soul would never be the same. That night had changed us forever. But it had been the following week when Poppy had died that made life unbearable. I'd understood why she'd done it. If I had been her, maybe I would have needed to do it too. Could she have survived if she hadn't taken the easy way out? I'd never know. The agony she had to endure would break anyone. But it hadn't just broken Poppy. It had ended her. She hadn't been strong enough to handle the repercussions of our stupidity.

Lifting my gaze from the worn cover of the book in my hands, I forced myself to look at Gunner as I said the words. They would spike through me as I said them. They always did. However, it was her story. One I wouldn't forget or ignore.

"She took her life."

I'm Not Really a Lawton

CHAPTER 21

GUNNER

Holy shit. The words sounded calm as she spoke them, but the look in her eyes made it seem as if they had been torn from her chest. Pain so intense it darkened the color of her blue eyes, making them almost black, as if her pupils had dilated, taking on the darkness of what she was saying.

"I'm sorry," I said sincerely. I would have never asked if I'd known the answer. I didn't understand how life could be so bad that anyone would want to end theirs. Things sucked but they passed and eventually they got better. You just had to hang in there and make it through. But I wasn't going to verbalize my belief to Willa. I had never known anyone who had taken their life. I didn't know what that felt like.

Obviously, from the expression on her face and depth of sorrow evident in her eyes, it wasn't something I ever wanted to know. I sure as hell wasn't asking any more questions about it. I wondered if I was the first person she'd told this to.

Was this why she had left Arkansas? To escape this reality. If one of my friends offed themselves, I'd probably need to leave too. But I wasn't sure where I'd go. Willa had a past to return to. All I'd known was Lawton.

The fact she'd shared this with me was big for her. I could hear it in her voice. She trusted me. Just like when we were kids. She knew I'd keep her secrets safe. Having her back made me feel less alone. Brady wasn't the same. Willa had always been the one I trusted above everyone.

"She didn't feel like she had another choice. I understand, even if I grieve for the loss of my friend every day."

The finality of what she had said was clear. She had told me all she was going to tell me, and I wondered why she had even given me that much if it hurt her so badly to talk about it.

We sat in silence for several minutes. Both lost in our own thoughts, and in a way it seemed this was a moment of respect for a life cut off too short. For whatever reasons.

"That's what haunts my eyes," Willa said finally. "What haunts yours?"

What haunted mine? What did she mean by that? No one ever asked me about my secrets. I didn't appear to be shouldering any. At least it hadn't been mentioned before.

"I don't know what you mean," I replied, even though the words didn't sound truthful as I said them.

She studied me a moment; the solemn expression on her face made me feel like squirming in my seat. As if she could read my thoughts and words weren't even needed.

"If that's what you want," she said simply.

Aggravated by the confusing turn of this conversation, I tried to remind myself not to snap at her. She'd just told me her best friend killed herself. Remaining calm, I replied, "What do you mean if that's what I want?"

"I know pain, and I recognize it when I see it in someone else's gaze. Your eyes speak for you. If you don't want to talk about it, I understand."

Well, fuck.

I couldn't continue looking at her, or I'd blurt out everything I never wanted anyone to know. Focusing on the view out the window just over her right shoulder was easier. I could get my head back together and think this through. Telling anyone this was making me vulnerable. Even telling Willa. But I wanted to. Needed to say it, and there was no one else on this earth I trusted to say it to. That had to mean something. Was this just friendship?

Was it me wanting what we had as kids? Or did I feel more?

My throat got tight just as the pressure began to ease from my chest.

"My father isn't my father. I'm not really a Lawton." The words exploded out of me as if the need to release them had a mind of its own.

Willa didn't looked shocked or horrified when I shot my gaze back to meet hers. There was also no pity in them. I hadn't wanted pity.

"That makes sense. You're not a coldhearted bastard." The casual way she said that made a smile tug at the corners of my mouth. I'd just told this girl my darkest secret, and she was making me smile.

"How did you find out?" she asked as if she had already known.

"I overheard my parents fighting when I was twelve. Shortly after you left. My dad hasn't been able to get an erection since Rhett was a baby. He had prostate cancer, and although surgery cleared him of it, his prostate was no more."

She let that sink in before responding. It gave me a moment to accept the fact my secret was out there. No longer guarded under Lawton lock and key. I'd shared it. I had just made my future vulnerable.

And I couldn't seem to give a fuck. I was relieved.

"Do you know who your father is?" she asked me. The curiosity in her gaze was almost funny. She liked the idea that I wasn't a Lawton. But then she'd never liked my dad.

I shook my head. "No. They don't know I know. I've never told anyone until now. Makes sense as to why they love Rhett more. He's the true heir to this shit, and he isn't a constant reminder that my mother had an affair and got caught."

Willa scrunched her nose. "You were the more likable son. I never understood their fascination with Rhett. Still don't. Even if he is a Lawton. They've not done much to make that a name to be proud of."

I agreed with her. Willa had been brutally honest as a child, too. She said what she was thinking, and you never had to wonder otherwise. Although sometimes you wanted her to keep her thoughts to herself.

"I'm sorry I didn't tell you I was leaving last night. I got in an argument with Brady about something stupid, and then I didn't want to go back into that crowd of people alone. I should have waited and told you though."

With all the truth being shared in this tree house, I'd forgotten about why I'd come looking for her today. She hadn't though. She knew why I was here.

"What did he do?" I asked, aggravated at the idea he had

fought with her. Asshole. Even more reason he shouldn't have let her run off.

She shrugged. "It's silly really. We just disagreed about the way he treats Ivy. He told me to mind my own business, and he was right. I should have."

The way she didn't meet my eyes told me she wasn't telling me everything. She could tell me that her best friend had killed herself, but she couldn't tell me what my best friend had done to send her running. I wouldn't push though. I'd just figure it out on my own. We'd done a fair share of opening up already.

"It's okay," I assured her. I wanted to warn her to stay away from Riley Young, but then she'd have questions about that. I didn't feel like talking about Riley right now. I needed to be alone for some time and sort through my thoughts.

It Was Better than Good

CHAPTER 22

BRADY

I didn't make it past the front of my truck before Willa opened the back door to her house. The cottage she lived in was small. Two bedrooms, one bathroom, a tiny kitchen area with a table in it, and a living room. When someone drove up out here, you heard it no matter what part of the house you lived in.

Willa loved her nonna's though. Or at least she had as a child. I didn't know her well enough now to know if that was still true. Maybe she had lived in a big house in Arkansas with privacy and missed that life.

"Nonna will be back soon. She won't like you being here. I'm a bad influence, and you're a good boy."

Not far off from the greeting I had expected. I didn't figure she was going to be happy about seeing me. Not after last night.

"I won't stay long. If Ms. Ames returns, I'll take the blame for being here and assure her you haven't led me astray in any form."

Willa had to have done something seriously wrong for Ms. Ames to worry about my safety around her beloved granddaughter. That was something to find out another day though. Not now with the kiss looking over our heads. I came here to apologize and hope we could move past it. I'd wanted to test things with Willa. And the test had been amazing. That kiss wasn't something I was going to forget. She was more than a childhood memory. She was worth knowing now. I wanted that.

She crossed her arms over her chest and scowled. She didn't want me here either. Talking about the kiss wasn't on her list of things she was ready to deal with. Too bad. We were dealing with it before we both faced Gunner tomorrow. He'd texted earlier that he wanted to talk to me. I ignored it because I wasn't sure what she might have told him today.

"You talk to Gunner today?" I asked her, cutting right to the point.

She nodded.

Shit.

"Did you tell him why you ran last night?" I couldn't bring myself to mention the kiss.

She shook her head. "No."

Whew. I had time to fix this before we had a fight that was pointless.

"I'm sorry . . . no, actually I'm not. I wanted to kiss you, and you kissed me back. It was good. It was better than good. It was fucking amazing."

The entire ride over here I had gone over what I was going to say, and this had not once been an option. Where the hell had all my blatant honesty come from? Seeing her face-to-face made me want to force her to admit she felt something too. Because I knew she did. That wasn't just all me.

Her cheeks turned a bright pink, and I wanted to grin, feeling a little smug that those words made her blush. But I controlled myself and waited on her to say something. Anything would be nice about right now.

With a deep sigh, she closed her eyes briefly, then shook her head. I'd forgotten how dramatic Willa could be. "We shouldn't be kissing. Maybe we were curious because of our past. I know I was, but you have a girl that you don't call your girlfriend, but she is something to you. I have a lot to prove and a lot to work through. I can't go around kissing guys."

"I wasn't suggesting you go around kissing guys last night. Just me." And the honesty just kept pouring out of my mouth like a volcano erupting. Damn it to hell. I had to shut up.

The frown on her pretty mouth deepened. I tried not to think about the way her mouth had tasted and how much I'd like to walk up to her and taste it again.

"You know what I mean. I'm not here for that. I'm here . . . I don't want that. I just want to go to school and make my nonna proud."

We weren't going to make any progress today because she wasn't going to explain any more. I could press, but she'd shut me out. The wall between us was growing higher by the minute, and I didn't want that. Not with Willa.

"Okay, okay. I get it. I didn't mean to send you running off last night. I am sorry about that. I shouldn't have lost you out there. I should have made sure you were safe. Riley Young sure as hell isn't safe for anyone to be riding around with."

She looked confused, then frowned. "How did you know I got a ride with Riley Young?"

Shrugging, I didn't see how this was a secret. "Gunner told me."

That frown just got worse. "I didn't tell Gunner about Riley. He didn't ask."

Ah, so Gunner hadn't wanted to explain his hatred for Riley. Couldn't say I blamed him. If she'd almost had my brother locked up behind bars for a false accusation, then I'd hate her that much too. I hated her enough now. Rhett was like my older brother or the closest thing I'd ever had back when he lived at home. Riley had come close to costing him his football scholarship and future in the SEC.

Rhett had been like the big brother to all of us once. He'd been the cool older brother we all knew and got us into the field parties before it was our time. We had all stood behind him back then, and Riley hadn't just become his enemy but all of ours.

"Gunner ran into her leaving the property on his way to find you when you ran off. I was in trouble with him for losing you, and he wasn't in the mood to run into Riley. Although he was relieved you were safely home, he hated that you were close to that bitch at all."

Willa stepped forward and shot me an annoyed glare. "Riley was nice, and she didn't do or say anything bad about y'all. I liked her."

With a warning she needed in advance, I made sure she understood me loud and clear. "Don't ever say that to Gunner. There is no one on this earth he hates more."

"His dad," she replied.

I shook my head. "Nope. Not even him."

"Nonna is on her way. She's already spotted you. Please go ahead and leave now so I don't have her angry with me."

I couldn't argue with that, even though I wanted to stay and talk. I didn't feel like I'd accomplished anything. Getting her in trouble with her nonna wasn't winning me any brownie points. But I wanted to hear her say she felt something too. That she wanted to try more with me like I did her. Even if there was a chance for more, I wanted to hear it.

I nodded. "Okay, but I'd like to talk about this again. I want more with you than friendship, Willa. If that's all you can give me, then I'll accept it, but that kiss hasn't left my mind one time since last night."

I didn't wait for her to respond. I turned and headed back to my truck, waving to Ms. Ames, hoping that helped out some with Willa.

I Didn't Think Chicken and Dumplings Could Heal That

CHAPTER 23

WILLA

Facing Nonna and letting her warn me to leave Brady alone was coming. Might as well deal with it and get it over with. It wasn't fair though since I hadn't asked him to come over, and I'd also asked him to leave.

I walked back into the kitchen and started fixing my late-afternoon snack. Nonna had run some food over to the big house for Gunner. She did that on Sundays since the Lawtons stayed gone all day and Gunner didn't participate in the Sunday ritual they had.

The back door opened just as I started slicing up a pear, and I inhaled deeply to calm my frustration with the lecture I was about to receive.

"Why was Brady Higgens here? Thought I told you to leave that boy be."

Here we go, I muttered in my head. I picked up the jar of peanut butter to spread some on my pear. "You did, and I've obeyed. Can't control Brady's actions though. He came over here, and I told him to leave. He never even made it to the back door."

Nonna was quiet a moment, and I didn't turn back to look at her. I made my peanut butter and pear snack as if it was the most important thing I'd done all day.

"Well, you weren't rude, were you?"

Was she seriously asking me if I was rude? Jesus, what in the world did she expect me to do?

"I asked him to leave. If that's rude, then yes, I guess I was." I still didn't look at her. I walked over to the freezer and got out a frozen mug for my milk.

"Why was he here?"

"Because I left the field party last night without saying good-bye, and he was worried he'd said something to offend me."

I didn't like lying. But at times like this it was necessary. My nonna could not handle the truth. *He kissed me, and I ran like hell* wasn't an option here.

She made a *hmph* sound that Nonna had perfected

over the years. "Well, that's nice of him. He's a good boy. No need to be rude when he stops by."

I wanted to growl my frustration. Another deep breath to calm myself was required here before I faced her finally. Holding my plate in one hand and mug in the other, I turned to meet her assessing gaze.

"I accepted his apology and told him it wasn't necessary and that he needed to leave. I was a bad influence and you didn't approve."

My mother would have yelled and lost her shit at a comment like that. But Nonna just sighed as if she couldn't do anything with me and shook her head. "Always so blunt and to the point," she muttered.

Yes, I was. And for the most part I was honest. Except when I had to lie about kissing Brady Higgens.

She waggled her finger at me. "I don't think you're a bad influence. You've just got healing to do over something that boy ain't ever seen the likes of. He ain't the kind that'll ever understand."

Although she was pointing her finger at me like I was a scolded child, her words helped. To know she didn't think I was too terrible to be around Brady the golden boy. It was for reasons that concerned me. Not him. She was worried about me.

My chest eased, and my frustration faded away.

"I know. He's a nice guy, but my demons are too dark for him."

Nonna looked sad. I wished I hadn't said that now. What I was thinking didn't always come out right.

She walked over to me and took my plate and mug from my hands, then placed them on the small linoleum table with the yellow chair straight out of the sixties that was the centerpiece of the dine-in kitchen. Then she turned back to me and pulled me into a tight hug.

"I love you, my Willa. You made mistakes and suffered greatly for them. I'll be here to help you heal. You're never alone."

Words a child expects from their mother. Words my mother would never utter to me as long as she lived. Words that reassured me that I was loved. My nonna was my safe place. She always had been.

"Thank you," I whispered into her shoulder, biting back the tears. I didn't need to cry anymore. I'd done enough of that.

"Why don't you share that snack with me. Then I'll fix us up a bowl of chicken and dumplings just the way you like them."

When I was a kid and things got tough or I was upset over something, Nonna always made me chicken and dumplings with more dumplings than chicken for a comfort meal. Thinking about having that meal now made me feel as if it would all be okay. Because back then it always was. But back then I hadn't suffered tragedy.

I didn't think chicken and dumplings could heal that.

"That sounds good," I told her instead of the truth.

She patted my back with reassurance. "Your momma don't know how to love the right way. Not sure why, because Lord knows I loved her and so did her daddy. But something in her never clicked right. She always put herself before all others. And I'm sorry about that, Willa girl. I'm really sorry about that."

Hearing her tell me what I already knew helped. It reassured me that it wasn't me that was unlovable, but it was my mother who just couldn't love me. I nodded, and she kissed my temple before pulling back and looking me in the eyes. "You're a special girl. One that makes me proud. Don't let life take that from you. Fight for it and prevail."

I wasn't sure what she meant by all that, but it sounded hopeful. It sounded like she believed in me. I needed someone to. "I will, Nonna," I promised her.

Later that evening as I lay in bed staring at the ceiling I realized a part of me was looking forward to going to school tomorrow. But when I tried to decipher what it was I liked most about school, I couldn't quite put my finger on it.

The idea of seeing Gunner in the morning and our ride to school or facing Brady again and listening to him say things to me he shouldn't. Both were pathetic, and I needed to stop pretending that there could be something like that for me.

Brady and his smiles that had made my heart go silly when I was a kid still caught me somewhere in the chest. He was so good and dependable. You could trust him and know he wouldn't let you down. He also had a girlfriend he wasn't actually claiming, so that was a strike against him. I wasn't sure if what I felt in that kiss was the little girl with the crush bleeding through or something more.

Gunner was different. He frustrated me and calmed me all at once. I didn't question his motives; I understood them. He didn't go out of his way to be kind to everyone, but he also wasn't leading any girls on. He was brutally honest. When I was with him, I got comfort I hadn't experienced in a long time. Part of me actually needed him.

I'd had a chance at being a normal teen, and I'd ruined that. *Demolished* was a better word. My choices were the things nightmares were made of.

Closing my eyes, I thought of the days after that night and the times I had tried to wake myself from the living horror I wanted to be only a nightmare. If I could just wake up and Quinn and Poppy would still be alive.

If only second chances were real. They weren't. They never would be. Not for me and not for Poppy.

My cell phone was tucked away in the antique maple dresser that sat directly across from my bed. It was there. I knew it was there. I just couldn't touch it or turn it on. My mother might have had the service turned off by now. I wasn't sure. I just knew I wouldn't use it again.

That small, flat smartphone held the memory of the last phone call I had accepted. A call from Poppy's mother. I never turned it back on again. I couldn't face the text messages or anyone else trying to call and find out details while attempting to act as if it was sympathy. That was the worst of it all. The nosy way people fished for the specifics.

Then there were the memories of the Snapchats and texts that I'd done daily with Poppy. There was too much on that phone that I couldn't see. I wondered if I'd always be this raw. Did a heart heal from something like this?

You're Not Dressed in Nineties Clothing

CHAPTER 24

GUNNER

Like the other times I had picked up Willa, she was waiting on me out by the road so I wouldn't have to turn into her drive. I had given her space after the way she had opened up to me about her friend. I was guessing that other than her nonna no one here knew that story. Everyone here assumed her mother had sent her packing and run off with a new man, since that was once her thing.

Telling me had been a big deal for her. Just as my telling her I wasn't really a Lawton had been a huge deal for me. I'd sworn to myself to never tell anyone, but I had wanted to tell someone. I had wanted to tell Willa. It was trust. I trusted her more than anyone I realized when the words fell from my lips. Why that was, I didn't really know. But I did.

I had placed a blueberry muffin on her seat. Not once had I forgotten to bring her whatever baked good Ms. Ames had on the kitchen table since the first day she'd ridden with me. I liked doing it for her, and I liked the way she smiled when it was there waiting on her. When she opened the door. She paused and saw it, then picked it up and flashed a smile at me.

"Thanks."

"You're welcome."

Also our normal morning greeting. I wanted this to become our routine. Mornings with Willa were better. I liked this. I got her alone, and we often laughed. Now we both knew the secrets we'd been trying to hide, and it felt more intimate. I'd never felt this connected to someone. From the moment I knew my life was a lie I had closed off, but Willa was reaching that part of me no one else had even tried to.

Once she was inside the truck and settled, she took a bite of her muffin and remained silent. I hadn't expected her to talk much this morning. Not after all we'd shared. I would let her have her peace and be patient. I wasn't going to allow her to pull away from me though. I needed Willa. And even if she didn't want to admit it, she needed me.

"I washed these blueberries for this muffin last night," Willa said as she finished off the muffin and brushed the crumbs from her hands.

"Then Ms. Ames should have left you a few in the kitchen this morning."

Willa nodded. "I completely agree. But Nonna won't bring home any food to eat that your parents paid for. Says it's stealing and the like."

That was ridiculous. Ms. Ames brought me meals from her kitchen when my parents ran off on Sundays and when she magically knew I needed a special treat. Our food was hers. "Hate she feels that way. I don't see it that way."

Willa shrugged. "Doesn't matter. I got the hookup with you, so it's all okay in the end." She was teasing. Her voice wasn't as heavy as the last time we spoke. There was almost a lilt in her tone that I remembered from years ago. As if that girl wasn't completely gone after all.

"True. Guess you better keep me around. I hear tell that the big house is getting strawberry hot cakes tomorrow."

Willa sighed. "Guess I know what I'll be washing tonight."

Again her tone was light, and I liked it.

"Just make sure you get them real clean. Hate to eat hot cakes with dirty strawberries."

Willa cut her eyes at me. "Don't push it. I may spit on the whole lot and not eat a one."

This time I laughed. Loudly. And her grin grew into a full-on beam. God that was nice. Real nice.

"I'll behave," I finally replied after my laughter eased. "You talk to Brady any this weekend?" I knew his truck had been up here briefly yesterday. This morning Ms. Ames had mentioned him stopping by and how that might be a bad idea. I should let him know Willa had healing to do right now.

I agreed with her. If Brady was coming around to be anything other than friendly, then he needed to move it right on along. The idea of that made me bitter, and I tried to bite it back. It was hard though. I had to remind myself Brady was my friend, the best one I'd had most of my life. Sure we'd changed over the years, but he was still important to me. We'd gone through a lot together, and that counted for something. I didn't want Willa to be what came between us, but then again I wasn't about to let him have her either.

"He came to see if I was okay with things yesterday."

Her answer wasn't as detailed as I wanted it to be.

"So he apologized?" I asked, pushing for more.

She shrugged. "Mmm" was her mumbled response.

We had told each other shit we hadn't told anyone else. We should be past this erecting-walls stage now.

"What kind of answer is that? Yes, no, shut the hell up I'm not telling you?"

A small laugh escaped her, and I was glad she found it funny.

"Yes and no. I was the one who ran, and I owed him an apology for acting the way I did." I wanted more than that. We were closer than this, and she knew it. My hands tightened on the steering wheel, and the idea that this was upsetting me so much shocked the hell out of me.

Besides, I disagreed. Brady had an easy life. The charmed sort. His parents loved each other, and his home life was secure. He hadn't dealt with family secrets or deaths. His aunt had been killed, but he'd hardly known her. Maggie coming to live with him had been the biggest drama he'd ever faced.

"But he did apologize?" I asked.

She nodded. "Yes, he just didn't need to."

I wouldn't argue on our ride to school. That thought I'd keep to myself. Brady, however, was going to get questioned when I had him alone.

"You're not dressed in nineties clothing," I pointed out, and she frowned like I had lost my mind.

"What?"

"It's homecoming week. Friday night is the homecoming game, and this entire week is themed. Nineties Day today, Western Day tomorrow, Pajama Day Wednesday, I forgot what Thursday is, and Friday is always School Colors Day."

She looked at my jersey and jeans. "You're not in nineties attire either."

"I'm on the team. I'm supposed to wear the jersey all week."

Willa rolled her eyes. This was silly. I was not participating in any of it. I'd have been surprised if she was. If I didn't get to wear my jersey every day, I wouldn't participate in that either. Who the hell knew what nineties was supposed to look like. We were barely born in the nineties.

"All we did for homecoming at my old school was a dance after the game and a big pep rally on Friday."

"We have those too. Except our pep rally is accompanied by a parade in the middle of town."

She laughed. "I had forgotten about the homecoming parade. Do y'all still throw candy? I used to love for Nonna to take me for the candy."

"Cheerleaders and band members do."

"Do we get out of school for this?"

"Yep."

"Sweet."

I'd asked Serena to homecoming two weeks ago because I knew she'd be a sure thing. After our win all I'd care about was getting some. Now I was regretting that. I wanted to experience it with Willa. I could always cancel on Serena, but then she'd make Willa's life hell. Something I wasn't selfish enough to do.

I'm Not Feeling the School Spirit

CHAPTER 25

WILLA

US Government was a good class to start the day with. It always felt like someone was telling me a story. No complicated math problems to figure out or Human Biology, which was the hardest elective they had available here, to concentrate on. Just a good story. If they would only let us drink coffee and eat muffins in class, then it would be the perfect beginning to the day. Unfortunately, Mr. Hawks was a stickler for no food or drinks in class. He also liked to see our hands moving and taking notes.

I didn't need notes. I was good with memory. I could listen to the story and remember all the details. Explaining that to him didn't seem like a wise idea, so I just took notes and wished I had coffee and muffins. I also wished that I wasn't thinking about who Gunner was taking to the homecoming dance. I was sure he wouldn't go alone. Brady would be taking Ivy. I didn't have to ask to know that answer. I wasn't available to date and do things like dances anyway. I had too much to prove and too much to find a way to live with.

Caring who Gunner took wasn't healthy, and I really shouldn't have. But while Mr. Hawks discussed foreign policy and national defense, I was thinking about a silly high school homecoming dance that meant nothing in the grand scheme of things. It was just a dance. Not one I needed to attend. I hadn't gone to my junior one either. Instead I'd been . . . drunk at a party.

Shaking my head to clear that memory, I focused again on Mr. Hawks and writing down what he had just said. This was all I needed to think about. Make Nonna proud and graduate high school. Then I was going to focus on proving to my mother I wasn't a loser with no hope, while helping kids not make the mistakes I did. If I could save one life from drugs and the horror they brought, then I would. Every life I saved, I'd be doing it for Poppy . . . and Quinn.

The darkness settled in my chest again, and I felt the sick ache in my stomach as I thought of them. Quinn's smiling face with her missing tooth. She'd just lost that front one and couldn't whistle anymore. We had laughed and laughed at her attempts. Quinn had been such a happy three-year-old girl. She had been closer to me than my own little brother, who stayed busy with after-school sports and our mother and his father. They had a family unit I was never really allowed into.

Poppy and Quinn had been my family. I swallowed against the lump forming in my throat. I couldn't break down in class. Listening closely, I wrote down every word out of Mr. Hawks's mouth. Making it a game to see if I could get it all down. That focus was the only thing that would get me through this class without crying.

"You okay?" Asa whispered, leaning over closer to me.

He had gotten into class after the bell rang, so we hadn't spoken, since Mr. Hawks had already started his lecture.

I'd completely forgotten him sitting there. I also hadn't ever gotten close enough to him at his party Saturday night to wish him a happy birthday. I would need to apologize for that. Sucking up my emotions, I managed a smile and nodded.

He didn't look convinced, and I was sure I wasn't completely masking my inner pain. Although I was trying my best. Mr. Hawks began writing our assignment on the video screen that now replaced the white board. This way he never had to get up out of his desk. He could sit down and type everything out. Note the sarcasm in my voice. His love for honey buns in the morning meant he needed to do a little more standing up.

"I didn't see you Saturday night," Asa said after Mr. Hawks was seated with a fresh cup of coffee and a honey bun.

"I'm sorry. You had so many people around you—then I left early. I'm not a real late-night person. I like sleep." That was the best lie I had.

He chuckled. "You're an interesting one."

I had no response for that.

"Did you get all those notes? I saw you writing like your life depended on it."

I nodded, then shrugged. "Well most of them. I tried."

He cocked an eyebrow and leaned toward me. "Can I borrow them? I was too busy watching you to get them all. Or any."

I started to nod when Mr. Hawks cleared his throat loudly, and we both turned our attention to the front of the class. He was glaring at us over his glasses with a bit of honey-bun sugar on his top lip. "Do I need to assign more work? Was that not enough?"

"No, sir, I think this will be just enough," Asa drawled,

sounding a little amused. I focused on my work in front of me and didn't look back his way again.

Asa laughed, but I didn't even smile.

When the bell rang, a guy sitting behind Asa started talking about the homecoming game, and I quickly snuck out. Surprisingly, there were a lot of oddly dressed kids in the halls completely on board with the nineties dress up. I thought a seventies day made more sense. They dressed cooler back then. This nineties thing just looked like a bad episode of *Friends*. It was my mother's favorite TV show of all time, so even thinking about the show brought up a slew of bad memories.

Brady was at the door when I stepped into the hall. His attention was on me, so he'd come simply to talk to me. I felt awkward around him, and I hated that. The kiss had changed everything, and I wished so badly he hadn't done it. It was easier with him before. I felt like I was hiding something from the world, and I didn't have the energy to have to hide anything more. I was hiding enough.

"Hey," he said, looking a little nervous. Great, he felt weird too. Even after our brief but uncomfortable talk yesterday.

"Hello," I replied, trying to think of something normal to say. A girl wearing a pair of overalls walked by with one strap undone and a crop top on underneath. That was a terrible look from the nineties, but she was spot on. Rachel from *Friends* had sported overalls more than once. Yuck.

"You not dressing up in nineties either? Y'all got the easy out with the jersey thing."

Brady was the quarterback. The school seemed to worship him, especially on game day. I didn't get that. Didn't it take a whole team to win a game?

He smirked and glanced around before looking back at me. "Yeah. You didn't dress up either. No school spirit."

"I'm not feeling the school spirit. Especially if that means dressing up in ridiculous costumes daily. I'll pass."

Brady's grin grew, then he leaned closer to me and whispered, "I don't blame you."

"You're the quarterback of this oh-so-special team. You should care," I shot back.

He didn't appear insulted. "I just care about winning. The silly shit I ignore."

That wasn't very Brady-like. Mr. Football Star. Just as I was thinking that, some random guy walked by and slapped him on the back. "Big week," he said, smiling at Brady like he could do it all. Throw the ball, catch the ball, and run it in for a touchdown. Terribly cliché.

I Don't Do Dances

CHAPTER 26

BRADY

Willa had loosened up a bit toward me in the hall earlier. I was now unable to wipe the grin off my face. Maybe I hadn't messed things up. I wanted a chance at this. At us. It was obvious she was trying to not feel uncomfortable around me after our kiss, and I was glad. Because I wanted more kissing. I wanted more Willa. I was currently ignoring the teacher's lecture while thinking of ways to get out of the homecoming dance with Ivy so I could take Willa. I was safe from Gunner taking her because he had already lined up Serena. I knew he wasn't willing to give up both a blow job and sex the night of homecoming to take Willa.

My only obstacle was Ivy, and I didn't want to be cruel.

I just wanted to be free of her. I had just let her be for so long I hadn't thought about what would happen if a Willa walked into my life. Hurting Ivy wasn't appealing, but as hard as I tried, I couldn't think of any other way. My mind went through several scenarios. It kept going back to me paying off Nash, who still hadn't asked anyone, to ask her to the dance. She'd tell him no, but then he'd tell her I was flirting with Willa, and to get me back she'd more than likely go with him. Making it her choice not mine, and she wouldn't be hurt.

That was just a lot of manipulating, and I wasn't completely okay with that, either. Dammit. Why had I asked Ivy? Though, honestly, I knew why. It had just been easy.

The bell finally rang, and that meant it was lunchtime. I was starving, but I was always starving. It was homecoming week, so the football players would get special meals brought in by the cheerleaders and booster club members. Today was pizza, and I was more than ready for it. Most of the cheer moms would bring in baked goods. I was hoping for some of those brownies with fudge icing that Ivy's mom always made. I mentioned them to her last week when she asked me my favorite dessert item for homecoming week. I'd been sure to request them.

Guilt gnawed at me again over the Ivy thing. I changed my train of thought and sought out Willa in the crowd.

My gaze fell on her and Gunner walking to the cafeteria together. I won't lie. A small bite of jealousy snapped at me. Gunner was laughing at something she was saying. The more I saw them together the harder it was for me to be around Gunner. I stayed irritated at him. He was leading her on. He wasn't a one-woman guy. Never had been. Willa was different. And so was my friendship with Gunner. It was slowly falling apart. Over her. And although that wasn't what I wanted, it was happening.

Willa was worth it. Watching her made me feel better. I liked the way she wore her Chuck Taylors with her skirts. It was cute. Almost as if she woke up deciding to dress girly, then saying screw it and throwing on her shoes before leaving.

"Mom brought your brownies," Ivy said as her arm slipped under mine and she wrapped herself around it. As if she was holding on to me for fear of falling. I felt a sick knot in my stomach because I wanted to be free of her, but I wasn't sure how to do it.

"Thanks," I replied, and I meant it. Knowing Ivy, she'd have me brownies every day this week. Once again proving what a dick I was for trying to get free from taking her to the homecoming dance.

"I also made sure that they got you cheesy bread with that sauce you like. I know you love it with your pizza."

Again there she was making me feel terrible. If she could just be the annoying clingy girl, it would be easier. But then she does nice stuff like this, and I feel bad.

"Great. Thank you," I said again.

We walked into the cafeteria with her still holding on to my arm in her very blatant sign that I was taken. Or so she wanted me to be. Not that the girls around here really cared. They would flirt with me just to piss her off. Ivy wanted a meaningful relationship. And I just didn't feel the same way about Ivy.

Turning my attention back to Gunner and Willa, I saw her sit down at our table with him. Interesting. Everyone on the football team got to invite one person to the table homecoming week to eat with them, and Gunner had chosen Willa. I had to choose Ivy. She'd made sure I had cheesy bread and brownies, dammit. Best I could do was go sit beside her. Which I hurried over there to do before someone else could. Ivy would have to deal with it.

"I swear to God! Not lost a homecoming since our freshman year and not about to start," Gunner was bragging to Willa. She glanced up at me as I sat down on the other side of her. Gunner was at the end of the table, and Willa was sitting to his right, on the side facing the door. I guess she wanted to keep her escape in sight if she needed to get away from all of us.

"Smack talk. I like it," I said.

Willa smiled at me. "This will be my first game. I hope y'all are right about all this football-god stuff. I hate to cheer for losers." The teasing tone of her voice made me break into a grin. That and the fact she was coming to our game. I hadn't expected that. My pleased smile began to fade as I considered who she might be coming with. I thought it was just Gunner I had to worry about. Was there someone else, too?

"Who are you coming with?" I asked, wondering if she had a date for homecoming and I missed it.

She shrugged. "Myself." Most girls I knew wouldn't be so cool with admitting they had no friends to go to a game with. The only two Willa had would be on the field. I hadn't seen any of the girls actually speak to her except Maggie. As if she had read my mind from across the table as she and West took their seats, Maggie spoke up. "You can go with me. I always need someone to sit with while West plays."

I wanted to high-five my cousin for being so awesome. A month ago she didn't even speak. At least not to anyone but West. To the rest of the world she was a mute. She'd come a long way.

"After the game you can ride with me and West to the dance, too," she added.

I liked that idea. Especially if I was able to end things with Ivy. Still trying to figure out how to do that without hurting her. She didn't deserve that.

"Oh, okay. But I wasn't planning on going to the dance."

Maggie didn't press that. She just nodded.

"You not have a date?" Nash asked, waggling his eyebrows like he was about to ask.

"No, but I don't do dances," Willa replied.

"I'm just glad you're coming to the game," I said, hoping to change the subject before it went in a direction I didn't want.

"What color is your dress, Maggie?" Ivy spoke up as her hold on my arm tightened.

Maggie shifted her gaze to Ivy, then glanced back at me. Maggie wasn't one for fashion talk. "Um, I don't know yet."

Mom was going to take Maggie shopping for a dress this week. Maggie hadn't pressed, and, to be honest, my mother was more excited than Maggie about getting her a dress. She'd have been fine wearing something she already had.

"Seriously? I've had mine bought since August. It's gorgeous with gold shimmer fabric that clings in all the right places."

I didn't respond and wiggled my arm free of Ivy's hold.

When she tried to hold on to it, I got annoyed. "I gotta eat," I told her, and then jerked it free. Sometimes it was hard to be nice to her. The hurt look in her eyes made me feel sick to my stomach though. Dammit.

You Gonna Feed Her Next?

CHAPTER 27

WILLA

Ivy verged on annoying. No. I was being nice. She annoyed me. Earplugs so I wouldn't have to hear her high-pitched voice constantly demanding the entire table's attention would be nice. I missed my picnic table outside, where I had been sitting alone with my brown-paper-bag lunch that Nonna packed me and my book. It was quieter out there.

Gunner had come after me and asked me to come eat with him, so I said yes without thinking that through. I'd been passing their table on my way outside for days now, and I knew it was full of people like Ivy who I didn't particularly care for.

Poppy would have started mimicking her by this point

while whispering in my ear. I'd be giggling and unable to control my laughs from escaping. My heart squeezed at the thought. I missed her.

"The dance is fun. You should go," Brady leaned down and whispered, then reached out to get a plate with cheese pizza and put it down in front of me. I only ate cheese pizza. There were three other choices being placed at the center of the table by what looked like overdressed mothers. I wasn't sure what that was all about. I didn't much care. What I did care about was that Brady had gotten me the correct one.

"Was that a lucky guess?" I asked him.

He flashed me a pleased grin. "No. I picked more than one pepperoni off your pizza back in the day Miss I-Only-Eat-Cheese-on-My-Pizza."

He remembered. The silly feeling in my stomach should have gone away, but it got sillier and I hated that I was smiling now. My gaze fell to his lips, and I remembered how they had tasted. How much I had enjoyed it. How much I shouldn't have enjoyed it.

"Didn't think I'd remember that? I don't forget much when it comes to you." His voice was still low so that only I could hear him.

"You gonna feed her next?" Gunner asked loudly, and we both jumped.

I turned my gaze over to Gunner, who had a smile on

his face as if he was joking, but it didn't meet his eyes. He was glaring with that grin, and his glare was centered on the guy beside me. Tension grew thick, and I no longer looked forward to that piece of pizza on my plate.

"Just being polite," Brady replied with a tightness in his tone that meant he knew Gunner was angry.

Gunner didn't answer that. He rolled his eyes and reached for a plate, then looked down the table before nodding his head to someone. I didn't understand him at all.

Seconds later I understood. Gunner had hailed him a female to entertain him with the nod of his head. A blonde with really long hair and boobs much larger than the average high school girl's sashayed up to him, and he pulled his seat back so she could sit on his lap. Disgusting.

"That should cause a riot with Kimmie," Brady muttered, and I turned my attention from Gunner and the girl to him.

"When he wants to cause a scene, he pits Serena and Kimmie against each other. It's his immature way of inflating his ego." Brady was whispering this so Gunner couldn't hear him. The Gunner I knew from the tree house wasn't this guy acting like a jock right now.

"Oh," I replied, unwilling to bad-mouth him. He was still my friend, and I obviously trusted him enough to hold my biggest secret.

Serena giggled loudly, and I heard Gunner's deep voice rumble as he said something to her in a low whisper. Jealousy slowly crept over me, and I hated it. I had nothing to be jealous of. Gunner was my friend. Keeping quiet and smiling at Brady or Maggie as they spoke to me was the best I could do. My emotions felt raw, and that was silly.

Lunch getting over couldn't be fast enough.

Ivy began to demand Brady's attention, and I focused on my pizza and wished again to be outside with my book at the picnic table. Once I finished my food, I would make an excuse to use the restroom, then bolt. I'd stay in there until the bell rang. I liked being alone. It gave me time to remember where I had been and where I needed to go. Being with Gunner and Brady made me forget at times, and I couldn't forget. It wasn't fair for me to forget.

Brady met me outside of our last period and asked me to sit with him, West, and Maggie. So I did. None of them mentioned my escape from lunch. Which was a relief. It made the last class speed by and kept my confusing thoughts off of Gunner for the time being. I had bigger issues.

I wanted to mention the fact I preferred sitting alone to Gunner when he gave me a ride home today. He'd been driving me home before his football practice this past week, but today they were having a break to rest after their big game this past weekend. So he wouldn't be rushing me home then leaving. I would have time to talk to him about it.

Maggie gave me her cell number before I left the classroom, and I explained I couldn't text because I didn't have a cell, but I could call her from my nonna's landline. Instead of looking at me like I had lost my mind, she smiled as if that made complete sense, and then we parted ways.

It wasn't until I was in the parking lot walking toward Gunner's truck that I realized it was gone. Glancing around, I looked to see if he'd moved it, but he wasn't here. He must have forgotten me. It was only six miles from here to his house. I could walk that.

Pulling my book bag up higher on my left shoulder, I headed out toward the main road. It was odd that Gunner had forgotten me. Almost as if he were angry with me. I had a gut feeling he was. The tension at the table during lunch had gotten thick, and I didn't know why. Sure, I was jealous of Serena, as much as I loathed to admit that. But I didn't say anything to him. He had no reason to be mad at me.

In the past eight months I'd dealt with far more important stuff than this. A guy leaving me to walk home wasn't a big deal. I would survive.

Hello, Son

CHAPTER 28

GUNNER

My brother's dark hair and hazel eyes were signature Lawton. He looked like our father. I, on the other hand, did not. Nothing like him. Which made sense, seeing as I didn't have any of his blood running through my veins. Rhett was sitting in the chair to my left. We were both in high-back brown-leather chairs that sat across from Father's desk.

Rhett had shown up at the school during last period, surprising me with his visit home. But he said we were meeting with Father at three and he had come to check me out so that neither of us were late. This had thrown me off. We'd never been summoned to the man's office like this. At least not together. This was weird.

"Did he know you were coming home?" I asked Rhett, who didn't seem concerned about this meeting.

He nodded. "Yes. He requested I return for this. I told him these were the only few days I had available."

Had he not questioned him about why we were meeting? "So you just came home because he said to?"

Rhett shifted in his seat, and this time he did seem a little nervous. "Yeah" was his simple response.

Because Rhett was the chosen one, he normally bucked our father at every turn. Coming home like this didn't seem like something he would willingly do. Unless there was something in it for him.

"He's late," I grumbled, hating the wait. I didn't like to talk to the man, much less sit in his office. A place I was never invited into. The walls were covered in bookshelves, and a painting that probably cost a million dollars hung on the wall over his desk. There were no family photos. Just one picture sat on his desk of him and Rhett last year at a charity event that he'd taken Rhett to but not me. Never me.

"You got something better to do?" Rhett smirked. That expression resembled our father so much that it annoyed me. I didn't want to dislike my brother because he looked like a man I hated.

The door opened behind us, and Rhett glanced back and appeared pleased that the sorry son of a bitch had walked into the room. I was just happy this would start so it could end. Being in here was uncomfortable.

"Hey, Dad," Rhett said so casually. They had a relationship that I didn't have a part in. Never wanted to either.

"Hello, son," he replied. That was also something that had once bothered me. Him referring to Rhett as son and me as Gunner or boy. Things like that had molded me as a child. Changed me.

Taught me not to trust or love. I had the old man to thank for that one.

"I'm glad you could be here on time, Gunner," he then said in the condescending tone he reserved for me and those he disliked. Fucker.

I glared at him with the most bored and uninterested expression I could muster but didn't respond to his comment.

"He was happy to come when I showed up to check him out." Rhett was trying to make this less tense, but it was pointless. Rhett had always tried to help me with our father. He didn't understand why I was the unloved son and he was the golden child. Even if he did, I didn't doubt his love for me though. Rhett had always been there for me as a kid.

With me and that man in a room together, tension was inevitable. I often wondered if he had figured out that I knew the truth. Overnight I had gone from the little boy trying to please him to dodging him at every turn.

"Of course he was," our father responded as if that was a bad thing and only proved my worthlessness. Truth was I'd much rather have stayed at school. Hell, I'd have rather someone poked my eyeballs with needles. That would have been more enjoyable than visiting with Satan.

"I have important matters to attend to this afternoon so let me get to the point," he began, looking directly at me as if daring me to speak or argue. As if I gave a shit what he had to say.

"Rhett is the Lawton heir. He has requested to receive the rest of his trust fund now in order to travel this summer in Europe with friends. I believe this is a reasonable request. He needs to enjoy the last few years of his youth before the pressure of this empire falls to him. I set up the trust funds for you both so that they would give you both an edge once you graduated college. I don't want to touch the investment now so I am going to give him part of his inheritance. Originally your mother had demanded it be equal between the two of you. I was young and agreed. However, things have changed, and with Rhett being the heir to what his great-grandfather built it is only fair that other than the trust fund set aside in your name, Gunner, you will not receive part of the Lawton wealth originally decided upon. I have changed the accounts, and that money is now safely divided between Rhett's investments and the money market account he currently draws from to live on."

As he spoke, my blood grew hotter, and the vein in my forehead that got pronounced when I was angry pulsed. I could feel it. Another thing that wasn't a Lawton trait. The emotions churning in me were still raw, but I'd managed to harden over the past few years. I wouldn't cry or beg for this man's love. Truth was I didn't want his damn money. Any of it. I'd leave this town and prove to him I could be more than some damn small southern town millionaire. I wasn't a Lawton. I was someone else, and I wanted to know who the fuck that was.

Acting as if I didn't know the truth had been to do what? Save me embarrassment? Protect my mother? She sure as hell hadn't tried to protect me over the years. Where was she now? At the country club sleeping with the tennis instructor? Unable to sit any longer, I stood and leveled my glare on the man I'd pretended was my father for years.

"I don't care. Rhett can have all that is yours. Even the trust fund you're allowing me to keep. This Lawton bullshit isn't mine. I don't want your name. I don't want your legacy. This family is a motherfucking joke. But I do want one thing—I want to know who my father is. I know you know. I know my mother knows. Either y'all tell me whose blood runs in my veins, or I tell this town that worships the family name that I'm a bastard from one of Mother's affairs."

There it was. Everything I'd ever wanted to say to him. I hadn't thought it out, exactly. I was more than positive Rhett didn't know any of this, and the fact he was okay with our father giving him everything made me question Rhett and where we stood. This wasn't my older brother who had always thought of me and fought for me. He was acting like our father in some way, and it hurt.

The man who had pretended to be my father my entire life stood up and held my glare with one of his own. "Who told you that? Did your mother?" His voice rose with each word.

I laughed. Not the amused kind of laugh, but the hard, bitter cackle of a man who had so much hate he wanted to taunt his opponent.

"You did. When I was twelve years old. Lowering your voice when yelling at my mother was never your strong suit."

"You'll not repeat a word," he threatened.

The manic laugh erupted again. "Really? And how will you stop me? Kick me out? That would be a great idea. I'll go pack my bags and start contacting all the news stations from here to Nashville with my story. They'll love this juicy Lawton gossip. The world will know you can't get a stiff dick anymore."

I enjoyed watching his face turn bright red. If he dropped dead of a heart attack right this moment, I would cherish it. Watching him die. I hated him that much.

"Jesus, Gunner, what is wrong with you?" Rhett finally found his voice and spoke up.

I didn't take my eyes off his father. Just in case he did die, I'd like to witness it. "You wanted it all, brother. You got it. It was never mine to begin with."

"This is crazy talk. I didn't ask for all this. He just decided to do it."

I had to look at him this time. See the lie in his eyes. "But you sat there quietly while he gave it all to you, didn't you? That's fine. I don't want to be you. I want to succeed on my own, not with the world given to me."

That was the truth. I had a lot to prove. To my mother, to this man in front of me, and to this town that believed me to be the spoiled heir to a fortune.

"Silence," Rhett's father roared.

While Rhett did as he was commanded, I turned back to him and smirked. "Or what? Think you can whup my ass? I'd like to see you try."

"You're as sorry an excuse for a human as your father was. Ungrateful, lazy mooch expecting the world to do as you wish. I kept you as my own and gave you a life he couldn't have given you. And just like him and your mother you took advantage of my generosity. If it wasn't for Rhett, I'd say your mother was the biggest mistake of my life."

"Dad! What the hell is wrong with you two?" Rhett sounded appalled.

"Keep talking, old man. Nothing you say matters to me. Tell me who my father is, and I'll leave quietly. Fight me on this, and I'll tell the whole motherfucking world the dirty Lawton secret. That I'm the bastard son."

The door swung open behind us, and my mother's voice sliced through the room. "No!"

Rhett spun around to look at her, his eyes still wide with confusion and shock. I kept my disgusted gaze on the man in front of me. He, too, was looking at my mother, but the threat in his eyes was clear. He expected her to shut me up. Good luck with that, asshole.

"Mom, thank God, they've lost their shit in here," Rhett said as if she were the salvation, not the cause of all of this. I should have known who my real father was. She hid me from him, and I hated her for that. She allowed me to be neglected by a man and verbally abused my entire life while all along there was a man out there who shared my DNA. I wanted to know him. I needed to know that something in him was good.

"Boys, leave," she said, her voice hard and cold. "Now."

Rhett did as she commanded, but I turned to face her. I wasn't going anywhere. "I think I'll stay," I replied, taunting her. She'd made this monster. Now she could fix it or at least give me my goddamn answers.

"Gunner," she sighed dramatically. "I need to speak with your father alone."

"He's not my father. Don't EVER call him that again."

She paused, and I expected her to argue with me, but she kept her angry glare focused on him. "No, he isn't. But you're a Lawton, and he knows it. You are heir to as much of the Lawton inheritance as Rhett, and he knows it. Now leave, and I'll remind him just how wrong he is."

"Don't call me a Lawton. His blood doesn't run in my veins." I spat the words out as if they tasted as bad as they made my stomach turn.

"That's where you're wrong. Lawton blood runs just as strong in your veins as it does in your brother's. Now. GO!"

Rhett's hand wrapped around my arm and jerked me toward the door. "Come on," he demanded, and I went with him. Not because I was obeying him. I was just confused. What the fuck did she mean I was a Lawton?

All. Of. It.

CHAPTER 29

WILLA

I opened the fridge and pulled out the plate of food Nonna had left for me. Grilled fish with steamed broccoli and a baked potato placed on one of her yellow flower dishes all wrapped up. I'd gotten home close to five after my long walk. That kind of physical exercise made me hungry. I was ready to eat all of this and a piece of pie.

The sound of a car pulling up outside stopped me from warming up my food. Setting it down on the counter, I went to the back door to see who was here. I had a feeling it was Gunner, but I wanted to see to be sure.

I was right.

Jerk.

I walked back to my food and unwrapped it, then placed it in the microwave. Just as the food began turning slowly inside on the glass platter, a knock sounded on the door. I debated ignoring him. He was coming to apologize. I expected him to. But I didn't have to forgive him.

When the ding of the microwave alerting me the food was heated went off, I reached in and got it out, then went to set it on the table. Another knock sounded. He wasn't giving up. I turned around and was going to give him an annoyed glare but paused when I saw the look in his eyes. He was upset. His eyes were bloodshot as if he'd been crying.

That got my attention. My annoyance was quickly replaced with concern as I hurried over to the door to open it and check on him.

"What's wrong?" I asked, not waiting on him to give me a reason why he was upset.

"Can I come in?" he asked, his voice hoarse from emotion.

I stepped back and motioned him inside.

"What's wrong?" I repeated.

He rubbed his face with both hands and inhaled deeply before looking at me.

"I know who my dad is," he said with such angst in his tone it almost didn't sound like him.

Oh. This wasn't what I had been expecting. At least

someone wasn't dead. Although the answer to this might be just as bad. It sure looked like it was. Asking him who didn't seem appropriate. So I waited quietly.

He took a few moments to stare off down my hallway as if he was still in shock. I wondered if he was even going to be able to tell me. This was bad. Hugging him didn't seem like the right thing to do either.

After what seemed like an eternity he turned his gaze to me. "I'm a Lawton after all," he said.

So his dad was his dad. Was that such a terrible thing?

"You aren't happy about that?" I asked.

He let out an empty laugh. "I'm a Lawton, but the man in that house is still not my father."

Now I was confused. Completely. Questioning him seemed like a bad idea, so I just waited again for him to decide how and what he was going to tell me.

"This is so fucked up." He sighed, running his hand through his hair with a look in his eyes that bordered on disbelief and anger.

Who the heck was his father? The suspense wasn't outweighing my concern for him, but I still wanted to know. He had me more than curious.

"I hardly knew him. There's pictures of me with him, and I could tell in the photos that he loved me. But I understand my father's hate for him now. The way my grandmother talks about him as if he were the devil. They hated him as much as they despise me."

I had to bite my tongue to keep from asking. That was insensitive. Unable to not do anything, I closed the distance between us and slipped my hand over his in a silent show of support. He turned his hand over and squeezed mine as if I were his only hope on a sinking ship.

"My grandfather wasn't my grandfather. Jeremiah Gunner Lawton was my biological father." He paused, then looked at me while his words rang in my head. "My mother slept with her father-in-law."

Oh God.

"It's all mine. He left it all to me legally. All. Of. It."

All of what? I wanted to ask, but I didn't.

"My father thought he could control my mother enough to hide the fact, but she stood there and threatened to announce it to the world and give me the means to go to court over it. The old man actually looked capable of murder. He threatened to send me off to a boarding school, and she laughed this crazed, manic laugh and informed him that if I chose to, I could have him removed from the house. Me. Remove that man from the house. Shit, Willa. What the hell? Am I even awake?"

I was beginning to think maybe I wasn't awake myself. I imagine he felt that way more so than me. "Is he still there?" I asked. I knew his hate for the man, and I wouldn't be surprised if he had sent him packing.

Gunner looked at me like I'd lost my mind. "I can't kick Rhett's dad out of the house. I don't want the world to know the truth. I'm not just a bastard. I'm my grandfather's bastard. Jesus this is fucked."

He had a point. This was fucked. Very much so. I tightened the hold I had of his hand. It wasn't much, but it was all the support I knew to give him. This time I stared off at nothing while the facts listed themselves in my head, and I was sure I wasn't dreaming. Gunner remained quiet as well. There weren't words for this really. My heart hurt for him. For the boy everyone thought had it all and the persona he'd lived his whole life. I wanted to hold him and fix it, and that emotion scared me. My feelings for Gunner ran much deeper than I had realized.

"Rhett left. He yelled and called Mom a whore, then left. She's locked away in her room crying now, and the asshole who is apparently my . . . brother, not my father . . . shit." He paused and shook his head at the thought. "He left the house too. The whole damn house has exploded."

The front door opened, and we both jerked our attention at the sound. Nonna was home. She was the only one who walked across the grounds and came in the front door. Especially unannounced.

I slid my hand from his, and he tucked both his in his pockets just before she walked into the kitchen. She looked at Gunner with compassion in her eyes. "Go on and y'all have a seat. I'll feed you your dinner here," she said, holding up a plate of food she'd brought back with her. "I reckoned you'd be here." She then finished, turning her gaze to me. She wasn't angry, but there was a gentle warning there. She'd overheard them at the big house. I wondered if she had known the truth. She'd been with them for so long, could secrets like that be hidden from her? I doubted it.

"Y'all go on and eat. I got some chocolate dream pie in the fridge. If'n you want to stay on the sofa tonight, it's yours," she said to Gunner, then went about the kitchen fixing glasses of sweet tea.

"Did you know?" Gunner asked her as we both sat down at the table.

She paused and didn't look back at us. Her attention stayed on the glasses in front of her. "Had my suspicions," she finally replied.

That was enough for him. He didn't ask more. We ate in silence, and when bedtime came, he slept on the sofa.

I Didn't Want His Life. Not Any of It.

CHAPTER 30

BRADY

Neither Willa nor Gunner were at school. It took me until third period to confirm this and then get concerned. Something was wrong. I tossed my books into my locker and headed for the back hall, where band and carpentry classes were held. No one would be there until after lunch today, and it had an exit door. The only one I could get out of and not get caught.

I texted Gunner once I realized he wasn't here, but he'd yet to respond to me. If he had just been absent, I wouldn't be worried. But him and Willa missing was something else altogether. It had to be a Lawton thing. Had they been caught together? Shit. Were his parents making Willa leave?

Or was it something worse? Was Willa consoling him over more crap from his father?

Regardless, I had to get there and check on them. Willa wasn't the kind of girl to skip school because she was hooking up. Something was definitely wrong with one or both of them. They might need me.

I ran to my truck, cranked it up, and headed for the Lawton property as fast as I could get away without attracting attention. Last thing I needed was for the cops to get me the week of homecoming. Not that they'd keep me from playing. Even the local police wanted a win.

If Coach found out me and Gunner were missing a day though, he would be pissed. I was going to have to get back before practice and so was Gunner. Whatever was happening couldn't be that severe. My temper started to rise as I imagined him and Willa messing around and getting caught.

He knew she was here because she had nowhere else to be. We didn't know why, but her mother was a bitch, so that was enough of an excuse for me. Willa hadn't opened up to me much, or really at all. Had she told Gunner things? The idea that he knew more about her past than me didn't sit well. Why would Willa trust Gunner over me? I was the trustworthy good guy. The one girls gravitated to when they needed a shoulder to cry on. Not Gunner. Never Gunner.

Turning into the Lawton drive that was lined on either side by oak trees, I grew more and more anxious. Surely there was a reasonable excuse, and we'd all be back in school before next period. Or at the latest, lunch.

Gunner's truck was parked in Ms. Ames's drive, so I pulled in beside him and cut the engine. They were together. But Ms. Ames was apparently allowing it, so it couldn't be too bad. I threw my truck door open and hurried up the walk toward the back door.

Several knocks later and no response. There wasn't even movement in the house. What the fuck? I reached for the knob to turn it, and, as suspected, it opened. There was no need to lock the doors here. To get on the property you had to know the code for the gate. It wasn't easy to get into the place.

"Willa?" I called out, stepping into the kitchen. It was silent.

"Gunner?" I tried, and waited. Nothing. The place was empty.

I walked through the house, checking for any sign of life, but it wasn't there. The sofa had a folded blanket at the end of it with a pillow as if someone had slept there. That wouldn't have been Gunner. Surely.

I exited out the front door and started down the steps and into the yard, searching for some sign of them when my eyes landed on the tree house. I hadn't been there in years. None of us had. It was our secret hiding place that wasn't so secret, seeing as Gunner's parents had had it built for Rhett when he was younger. But we liked the privacy we thought we had there.

I began walking that way without thinking about it. Something in me knew they were in there. Why they were in there I wasn't sure, but I knew they were. It was where we had always found each other when we were younger.

When I stopped at the bottom of the tree, I heard Willa's voice first. Taking the steps one at a time, I climbed up to join them.

Gunner's eyes were the first to make contact with me. "Hey" was all he said. Something in his eyes was empty. More so than normal. That worried me.

"You okay?" I asked, walking inside without having to bend over. I'd forgotten how elaborate this tree house was.

He shrugged, then his gaze swung to Willa's. "Am I ever?" was his response.

I turned to look at Willa, and she was studying her hands that she was fidgeting with in her lap. This was going to take a while. I sat down on the wooden bench that lined the wall across from them.

"So, I take it this has something to do with you, since Willa looks unsure and nervous," I said, glancing at Gunner.

"It wasn't at all suspicious that you both weren't at school. And it's homecoming week at that."

Willa finally glanced up and looked at Gunner with compassion. Okay, so something was really bad here. "Gunner, what is wrong?" I asked.

Gunner met Willa's gaze for a moment, then turned to me. "Family shit. My father wants to give Rhett everything. My mother is furious. Lots of yelling and fighting. Rhett left and hasn't returned my calls."

Well hell. That sucked. Life for Gunner had mostly always sucked at home. He had never had it good there. That was something I never envied of Gunner. I hadn't asked about his home life in years. Somewhere along the way our friendship had changed. We talked football and girls but nothing deeper. Willa coming back had given him something he and I had lost. A real friendship. The jealous bite that caused made me feel guilty. He had needed someone, and she'd been there. I hadn't.

This was typical of his sorry excuse for a dad, but I hated he was dealing with it. "You stay at Ms. Ames's last night?" I asked, remembering the blanket and pillow on the sofa.

He nodded. "Yeah. Couldn't go home."

Willa remained quiet as she sat there. I was torn about her being who he had run to. Being jealous of Gunner telling her instead of me. But was it because I wanted Willa or she was stepping in on my friendship? I wasn't really sure.

When she'd come into our lives as kids, I hadn't liked her right away. Gunner had liked her too much, and I didn't want her taking my friend away. Over time we'd all become close, and I'd wanted Willa around just as much as Gunner. But we weren't kids anymore.

"You coming to practice today?" I asked him.

He nodded. "I need to hit someone. We were both going to check in right before lunch. I just needed some time this morning."

I could understand that. Gunner's relationship with his parents had never made sense to me. My mom and dad were always there when I needed them and even when I didn't. Mom made cookies and let me have the guys over to watch the game videos. Dad was always there cheering me on and believing in me. I was who I was because of my parents. That's why I always understood Gunner's stupid decisions. He was who he was because of his.

I was lucky in ways Gunner would never experience. Money wasn't everything in the world. Being friends with Gunner had taught me that. I didn't want his life. Not any of it. No amount of money and power made that life desirable.

"You know you're welcome at my house any time you

want. I've got two beds up in that attic room of mine. One is yours if you need it. Just say the word. Mom would love to stuff you with cookies."

A smile tugged at Gunner's lips. "Thanks. I'll remember that." For the first time in years I felt that old friendship ease back into place. The one where we knew we had each other if we didn't have anyone else. And it always made it all right.

I stood up, walked over, and slapped him on the back. "If you need to talk, I'm here."

Gunner nodded.

I glanced over at Willa, who was watching us both. "You need a ride to school? Or you going to stay with Gunner until he comes?" I wanted her to ride with me so we could talk. About Gunner and the possibility of me taking her to homecoming. I wasn't sure where she stood with Gunner. I didn't think he was ready for serious or ever would be. If this was just a friendship with them like we all once had, I wanted to explore more with her. I was going to break it off with Ivy today. She'd texted me fifteen times last night and called ten. She was out of hand, and I needed to end things.

She looked at Gunner for an answer. I didn't want that to sting, but it did. Guess I was jealous of her giving him attention after all.

"She'll come with me," Gunner piped up.

It wasn't like I could push it. Gunner was having a hard time, and he wanted Willa to make him feel better. I just didn't like the idea of him hurting Willa for selfish reasons. Using her for someone to listen to and lean on but not giving anything back in return. She'd been hurt. It was obvious, and Gunner had too much emotional turmoil to help someone else with theirs.

"I'll see y'all at lunch then" was all I could say before I turned and headed back down the ladder. If she wanted him, I couldn't stop it, but I was afraid he wasn't going to want her the same way.

Next Time Though I Won't Let You Run

CHAPTER 31

WILLA

I understood football and the need to win, but I didn't think Gunner really had to go to practice today. However, I wasn't going to tell him that. Not with the mood swings he was dealing with. The best I could do was listen to his rants. No advice or consoling. My just being there was all he seemed to need last night and today. So even when Brady had come to check on things, I'd stayed silent.

This wasn't my nightmare. It was Gunner's. All I was offering was my ear. And that was all he had asked for. Brady, on the other hand, he didn't trust, or he didn't want him to know. Because he'd gone beyond evading the truth;

he'd just lied to him. I wasn't sure how I had been the one he trusted with this truth. Maybe because I'd told him mine. But for whatever reason, I was going to be worthy of his trust.

Brady hadn't been surprised by the less-than-half truth he'd been told. Which only confirmed the ass Gunner's so-called father was. Brady had seen more than I had over the years. I would think Gunner would want to share with him more than me. That hadn't been the case though.

We didn't make it to school by lunch, but we did make it in time for the class right after it. The office seemed okay with our excuse, and because I was with Gunner, I think it helped my reasons. If I hadn't been, I was sure they'd have given me break detention or something.

It wasn't until we were walking to class that Gunner realized he had forgotten me yesterday. With all that had happened, I'd forgotten myself.

"Shit," he said, stopping in his tracks and slapping his forehead. I thought he'd forgotten homework or his football jersey.

"What?" I asked.

He looked at me with a frustrated frown. "How did you get home yesterday?"

"Walked."

"Fuck," he muttered. "I'm sorry, Willa. Rhett checked

me out to meet with my dad, and that was so unexpected I forgot completely."

I shrugged, because compared to his last twenty-four hours the fact I had to walk home was really no big deal at all. Especially after all he'd been through, I didn't want him feeling bad about me. If I could fix all his problems, I would. I tried not to think too deeply into that though.

"It's fine. Your day was tough, and it was good exercise for me."

He shook his head, still clearly annoyed with himself. "I won't do it again. I swear."

"Really it's not a big deal. I enjoyed the walk." Which wasn't exactly true, but there was no reason to make him feel worse about it.

"Stop trying to make me feel better. Ain't going to work," he grumbled.

I didn't have a real response to that, so I said nothing.

He walked me toward my classroom, but before we even got five doors close to it, he stopped and opened a door to a dark room, then reached for my arm and pulled me inside.

"What," I said, confused, as the door closed behind me.

Gunner's grip released my wrist; then his hand slid up to cup my face. The light from the hallway barely gave me enough illumination to see. But I saw Gunner's face as he leaned into me. I knew what was coming, and my stomach did a flutter of excitement just before his lips landed on mine.

Softly he brushed them back and forth over mine. The gentle touch brought a sigh from me that Gunner used as an opportunity to slip his tongue past my lips to tangle with mine. My hands found his upper arms, and I held on to him or drew him closer. I wasn't really sure with the fireworks of electricity going off in my head.

This I hadn't expected, but I didn't want it to end. The peppermint taste of his gum mingled with mine, and I leaned in closer to breathe him in. His hard chest pressed against me.

Cold air met my now damp, swollen lips. And my eyes flew open to see Gunner stepping back away from me. His eyes were on me with a surprise that I understood because I felt it too. There had been a connection there that made me want to pull closer to him. Soak him in and never let go.

I felt complete.

I was an idiot.

Because just as I thought all of this, Gunner opened the door and left me there. Alone in the dark.

Running off after kissing wasn't a good sign. It was exactly what I'd done to Brady. Was this my payback? The universe showing me how this feels? Because if this was how Brady felt, I owed him a much bigger apology. This feeling wasn't one I wanted to repeat. Ever again. Kissing Brady had been nice. Kissing Gunner had rocked my world.

It was Brady who met me by my locker at the end of the day. "Gunner asked if I could give you a ride home. He had something he needed to do before practice."

His something to do was avoid me. That hurt. A lot.

I nodded and swallowed the lump now forming in my throat. "Okay, thanks. I can walk if you need to get to practice."

He shook his head. "No. I've got plenty time."

I doubted he had plenty time, but I couldn't argue because my stomach was in knots. I just wanted to get home. Back to my bedroom. Alone. Where I should have stayed instead of opening up and forming friendships again. Especially with Gunner Lawton.

"You okay?" Brady asked, and I lifted my gaze to meet his. I couldn't tell him what was wrong with me.

"I'm good," I said, forcing a smile.

He didn't look convinced. We walked outside toward his truck with some small talk, and just before we got to his truck, I turned and looked at him.

"Brady," I said, needing his attention.

He glanced over at me. "Yeah?"

"I'm sorry about running off after you kissed me. That was rude and I . . ." Pausing, I wasn't sure what my excuse for it was, but I had to say something. "I just wasn't expecting it, and because we're friends it scared me."

A slow smile touched his lips. "That's okay. Next time though I won't let you run."

There wouldn't be a next time. I knew that because my heart wasn't in it with Brady. He was a childhood crush and a friend. Nothing more. I knew now what the real thing felt like, and what I'd felt for Brady wasn't the real thing.

Good Ole Stable Brady

CHAPTER 32

GUNNER

I sat in my truck after practice for thirty minutes, staring at the clock. Ms. Ames had said I could come to her house again tonight, but I wasn't sure I could face Willa. Not after that kiss. Jesus! That kiss was more than I'd expected. It was terrifying, and I had enough shit in my life right now. I wasn't prepared for the impact of one simple kiss. My head and heart were not ready for Willa Ames. She scared the hell out of me.

I was going to Brady's. I'd send him to get Willa in the morning or some shit like that. I needed space from her. It was a dick move, but she had messed with my head. That didn't fit into my world right now. I had family lies and dirty money and a mother who I never wanted to lay eyes on again.

Willa had been through her own hell, and I wasn't what she needed. Brady was what she needed. Good ole stable Brady. And I knew he wanted her. That plan sounded like a winner to me. Brady could be her strong shoulder to lean on, and I could go on about my life living through my own mess. No need to add hers to it.

After convincing myself I would be fine if Brady went after Willa, I cranked the truck and headed to the Higgens' house. Coralee would have cookies and milk. That sounded pretty damn good about now.

Blaring the music as loud as it would go helped drown out my thoughts. Especially thoughts about Willa. She didn't fit into my world right now. Probably never would. I needed the Kimmies and Serenas of this world. Not the Willas. They were too much. They wanted too much. They needed too much. All of which Brady was good at giving. I had never been that guy, and I never would be. Probably because of my breeding. Hell, I was my grandfather's son. How fucked up was that?

When I was a kid, I daydreamed about having Brady's life. His family. I wanted that. It was a fantasy, of course, because that kind of life didn't live within the Lawton world. We were all pretending. It was what we were trained early to do. Act as if things were perfect.

Well fuck all that. It wasn't perfect, and my life sucked. I wasn't pretending like being a Lawton was a good thing. I wasn't conforming to this bullshit life.

Brady's truck was in his drive, and so was West's. He was here for Maggie. They were together all the time. It verged on annoying. No, it was completely annoying.

I hadn't brought an overnight bag, but I figured I could use Brady's crap. Wear his clothes. I wasn't going to that house, and Ms. Ames would have brought my things to her house, but I couldn't go there, either. I should have called her so she wouldn't worry, but the fear that Willa might answer kept me from it. Maybe later I'd call. If Willa answered, I'd just ask to speak to Ms. Ames. Act like nothing happened.

We all knew I was the crown prince of pretending.

Brady's mom, Coralee, answered the door. She was the mother I never had.

"Well, Gunner, it's good to see you. Come on in. I just took the others some snacks. Chocolate chip cookies fresh out of the oven."

Just what I wanted to hear.

"Thanks, Mrs. Higgens," I said, and she patted my back in her maternal way as I walked past her, towering over her by at least seven inches.

"They're in the den about to watch last week's game, again," she added with an amused sigh.

We often watched our games from the past week over and over to improve on things we messed up and perfect things that were working. That would help get my mind off things. I loved this house.

"Okay," I replied, then headed to the den, where I could hear Brady's voice rising as it did when he got excited about a play.

"I'm not saying it's bad. I'm saying if we take it in closer and tighten it, then we could demolish the Trojans on Friday night" was Brady's argument when I walked into the room.

"And I'm saying it looks as tight as we can get it," West replied, sounding annoyed.

"Could y'all just eat the cookies and stop arguing over this?" Maggie piped up.

"I'll eat the cookies quietly," I added to the conversation, and all three pairs of eyes swung to me.

"Gunner, good, you're here. Listen—watch this play and tell that hardhead it can be tightened up and we can pull in Nash for the snap." Brady looked passionate and fired up. That was why he was going to an SEC college and making a career out of the game. He saw what everyone else didn't.

"Can I have cookies first? Your momma said they're still warm."

Maggie laughed, and Brady rolled his eyes. "We have a game to win Friday night, and you are worried about cookies."

I nodded. "Yes, I am."

Maggie pointed to the table where Coralee had left a large tray of cookies, some small sandwiches, and a bowl of barbecue chips. I made my way over to it and got three cookies for good measure and poured myself a glass of milk out of the bottle she had sitting in ice. Coralee Higgens was like Martha Freaking Stewart.

Brady sighed dramatically and dropped down onto the leather chair behind him. "I give up," he groaned.

"Does that mean we can watch an episode of *Fuller House*?" Maggie asked in a tone that wasn't serious. She was teasing her cousin.

"What the hell is *Fuller House*?" Brady asked as I walked over to sit in the other empty chair.

"*Full House* all grown up," Maggie explained.

"*Full House*, that show from like the eighties or something?"

Maggie nodded. "Yep."

That just got another irritated groan from Brady.

"He's focused on winning. It makes him moody," West

told Maggie as he held her hand in his. I'd call him a pussy, but the dude had lost his dad recently and Maggie had helped keep him together.

"You seen Willa this afternoon?" Brady asked as he turned his attention to me.

I did not want to talk about Willa. I shrugged. "Nope. Haven't seen her since we got to school."

Brady frowned. "She seemed upset after school. I was wondering if she'd said anything to you. She promised me she was fine, but she wasn't. I wonder if the crap she's dealing with from her home is bothering her."

Guilt. It ate through me like a painful stab in the chest. She was upset over the kiss and my leaving her. I did that. Not what she'd dealt with at home but what I'd done to her. I was a jerk. She knew that now.

I wanted to be all she needed, but I couldn't be. I was too broken myself. I didn't trust myself with something as precious as Willa's heart. I'd been a screw-up my entire life. Acting out for attention and getting the wrong kind. Willa needed more than me. I wanted her to have the best. I wasn't even a tenth of what she deserved.

"She seemed fine to me today" was all I said. "Let's see that play, and I'll give you my opinion," I said, changing the subject off me and Willa. I didn't need Brady thinking anything happened. He'd just make me feel worse. Besides, she needed him, and he didn't need to be thinking about her kissing me.

Brady jumped up and grabbed the remote. "Watch the left side," he said enthusiastically.

"Here we go again," West grumbled.

I Don't Hate You

CHAPTER 33

WILLA

The phone rang, and I almost didn't answer it. The last call had been from Gunner, who hadn't said anything to me but had asked to speak to Nonna. Apparently he was staying the night at Brady's. I didn't have to wonder why. It was obvious he was avoiding me. I'd be getting up early in the morning and going to the bus stop. I knew without asking that Gunner wouldn't be coming to pick me up. The kiss had sent him running. Fine. Whatever. It would never happen again.

Kissing Gunner had shown me what I had been trying to ignore. He was the boy who had my heart now. Not Brady. But I couldn't force him to want me. I would let him react however he needed. I understood hiding from life. I'd done it myself.

"Get the phone," Nonna called from her bedroom. I had no choice now. I was going to have to answer the stupid thing.

Taking a deep breath and reminding myself if it was Gunner I couldn't curse him out because he was dealing with a lot right now, I reached for the phone.

"Hello."

There was a pause, and I almost said hello again; then he spoke.

"Will." My brother's voice startled me, and I froze. He hadn't spoken to me in over six months. Even when I had called and written, he'd ignored me.

"Hey, Chance." The happiness from hearing his voice felt foreign. I wasn't used to that much joy anymore. It had been too long.

"Hey." He sounded nervous, but there was happiness in his tone too. "How is Nonna's?"

He barely knew Nonna. She hadn't been around him much of his life. Our mother didn't bring us to visit. Nonna had to save up to come visit us when we did see her. "She's good. Still baking pies and working at the big house."

"Cool. Um, so are you liking it there?"

I wasn't sure anymore. If he had asked me yesterday,

I'd have probably been able to say yes. But after today, and hearing his voice, I was now missing him and my life there badly. Maybe not my mom but the life I'd once had.

"Yeah, it's good. I miss you though."

He was quiet a moment before saying, "I miss you too."

My chest ached for two reasons. One, because I did miss him terribly, and two, because he was talking to me again. I had feared I'd lost him. He only knew what he'd been told about that night. No one really wanted to hear the truth. Even though the truth wasn't much better. In the end Quinn had drowned. That was the outcome of our mistakes. Mistakes we could never take back.

The image of Quinn's small, lifeless body floating upside down in the deep end of the pool still gave me nightmares. I hated to remember. The reality of it chilled me to the bone.

"How's school?" I forced myself to say as my throat tightened and my horror returned.

"It's okay. Mom's pregnant. She's having a girl."

Those words came out all rushed and nervous. Like he was almost yelling them before he lost his courage.

Our mother was having another baby. A girl. To replace me. Chance might not understand that, but I did. I was her mistake. The obstacle that stood in the way of the life she had dreamed of. I was never the child she wanted. She left me with her mother the majority of my life. I was a disappointment, much like she had been to Nonna. So she was having a redo.

"Tell her I said congratulations," I told him. "I'm sure your dad is excited."

"Yeah," he replied, not sounding so sure. I wondered if they were fighting a lot in front of him.

"Are you excited about the baby?" I asked.

"I guess. Don't they just cry a lot?"

Smiling, I remembered the little time I got to spend with him when he was a baby. I was amazed by him, but we never lived together until he was eight years old. I loved him though.

"You'll love her. I remember how fascinated I was with you and how your crying didn't bother me so much because when you were happy and laughing, you were the cutest baby I'd ever seen."

"Really?" There was a smile in his tone.

"Yep. I thought you were great. Still do."

He didn't say anything right away. I gave him time to work through his thoughts. "I'm sorry I haven't called you."

He was a kid. With two parents who hated me. That wasn't his fault. "It's okay. I understand. I made big mistakes, and you not wanting to talk to me made sense. There were times I didn't want to even look at myself in the mirror. But I've missed you and thought about you all the time."

"I think about you too. I miss you reading Percy Jackson to me at night. Mom won't do it."

Chance was dyslexic and he loved books and reading, but it was so hard on him it took him hours to read a couple pages. So at night I used to read him a chapter from the new Percy Jackson novel he would get from the library at school. It was our thing. I missed that too.

"I miss reading to you. Have you been keeping up your own reading?" I asked.

"Yeah, I'm trying. I made an eighty-five on my literature test." He was so proud of himself.

"That's fantastic! I'm so proud of you."

"I smoked pot with George Hasher last week," he added, and my stomach dropped.

Shit.

"Chance," I said slowly, trying to figure out what to say to him. After all that had happened to me, I thought he'd never touch the stuff.

"I wanted to understand why you did it."

That hurt. More than he would ever know. I put a hand on my stomach and sat down in the nearest chair. My knees were slightly weak, and I was sick.

"Because I was stupid. That's why I did it, and my stupidity changed my life. In a terrible, terrible way." Not that I had to tell him this. He already knew.

"I know," he said. "I just wanted to understand . . . things."

He wanted to understand how Poppy and I could have forgotten about her little sister long enough for her to fall in the pool, hit her head, and drown. The autopsy revealed she'd been in the water for over an hour. There had been no saving her. Poppy hadn't been able to live with the guilt and pain. So she'd done the only thing she knew to do. She'd taken her own life days later.

"Did it help you?" I asked while wanting to scream at him to never do it again. He needed to know how it ruined lives and ended them. It wasn't safe and fun. It was evil. I learned in a way I never wanted Chance to experience.

"Yeah, I didn't care about anything. I thought life was hilarious. It was freeing, but I get how that is dangerous. I won't do it again."

Good. Relief rushed through me. I didn't want Chance to suffer what I would never be without. Regret, guilt, loss, emptiness. Those would follow me my entire life. Because I had wanted to be high and drunk with friends. We had so stupidly thought staying at home made us safe. We weren't driving or in an environment that could harm us. But we hadn't considered that a crisis could happen and we'd need to be alert enough to deal with it. Even at home.

"I don't hate you," Chance said, and tears burned my eyes.

"Good, because I love you more than life."

"I love you too."

I Had to Let It Go

CHAPTER 34

GUNNER

I had avoided her for four days. I hadn't even made eye contact with her. It was game day, and I had one focus in mind. Winning the game. Once we had won, I was taking Serena to my truck and spending several hours. It was homecoming, and I was ready for it.

Walking out of my second period, Asa and Willa were directly in my path talking. Willa was smiling up at him, and I watched them closely. When had Asa and Willa become so chummy?

"I'll see you at lunch," he said as I got closer to them.

She turned to leave, and her eyes met mine. For a moment there was a flash that one could have mistaken for her being pleased. But then they went empty, and she walked away as if I hadn't even been standing there. That burned. I'd asked for it, but it still motherfucking burned.

"What's up with you and Willa being so buddy-buddy?" I asked Asa, unable to pretend like I didn't care. Where the fuck was Brady? He had a wide-open opportunity here, and he was blowing it.

"Taking her to the dance tonight," he said, beaming like he had won the lottery.

"I thought Brady was," I said, not really knowing if that was even close to true. I just assumed Brady would ask her.

Asa frowned. "Naw, he's taking Ivy."

He never got the nerve to dump Ivy. Well, then he deserved this. He could watch Willa dance with Asa and sulk all night. I wouldn't be dancing. I had other plans. Ones that didn't make me think about my parents and my house I still hadn't been back to.

I was going to have to go home after school though. I had to get my shit for tonight. Hopefully neither parent would be there. Rhett still was ignoring my calls and texts. I was trying not to let it get to me. But it was. We'd always been close. This had to have been hard for Rhett to hear. I'd known most of the lies for years. But I couldn't talk to him and check on him if he wouldn't return my calls or texts.

Brady stopped Willa, and I watched them. He was all smiles, and I knew he was liking the taking-her-to-school thing. He left earlier and always spent more time on his appearance. Why he let Asa get a chance at her I didn't understand. He obviously hadn't kissed her yet. Damn, that kiss. It was in my every thought. I was dreaming about it. That kiss was controlling me, and I didn't even care.

"I'm picking her up for school starting Monday. I asked her, and she said yes. Glad you decided to toss that job off to a taken guy so I had a chance."

Shit.

What was Brady's deal?

"You don't even know her." My comment sounded more annoyed than I had meant it to. But whatever.

Asa shrugged. "Gonna get to know her. I like what I do know."

She had hell in her life he couldn't even begin to understand. It wasn't my place to tell him, and her secrets would remain that. Her secrets. I'd protect them.

"Don't hurt her." Okay, that came out as a warning. What the hell—it was.

"Don't plan on it. Jesus back off. I like her."

The urge to slam my fist into his face was strong but not the best move. I knew Asa. We were friends. He was a good guy. I was being ridiculous and maybe a bit jealous. I had to let this go. I wasn't going to ever have a real relationship, so I wasn't ever going to have Willa. That kiss . . . well, it was my warning. That I couldn't even have a small taste of her. I was too fucked up.

She needed a Brady Higgens, dammit. Why wasn't he taking advantage of this? God, he was a dumbass. He didn't even like Ivy.

West used to help keep Brady's head on straight, but lately Maggie was all West could think about. I wonder if the first time he kissed Maggie he'd felt the earth move. That would make sense as to why he became so attached to her so quickly.

"I'll see you at lunch," Asa said with a look of annoyance at my ignoring him, then left me there. Thinking about the reasons why that kiss with Willa couldn't mean more.

In my avoiding-Willa plan I hadn't been faced with her sitting at my lunch table with the team. And Serena all but perched on my lap. This was awkward. It hadn't been before, and that stupid kiss had made it this way. Thankfully, Asa hadn't taken a spot close to me, so I didn't have them directly there beside me. After my comment in the hall earlier, Asa had made the move to sit down the table closer to Nash and Ryker. West and Brady were the two closest to me. Which meant Ivy and Maggie were also. It was obvious that Maggie wasn't a fan of Ivy or Serena, so she didn't appear comfortable.

Ivy was chattering on about those stupid brownies her momma made for Brady like she was the best girlfriend on the planet, and I tried to ignore her by straining to hear what Asa and Willa were talking about. Interestingly enough, so was Brady. He wasn't paying any attention to Ivy either. And I could tell he felt guilty about that. Which made no sense. In the least. Why was he even wasting time with her? I never understood that.

"Brownies are good, but not much beats those cookies of Mrs. Higgens's," I said, wanting to shut the girl up so I could hear Willa.

"I second that. Those cookies are incredible," West agreed.

Ivy shut up, although she looked ready to toss us both across the room. I watched as Willa tucked a strand of her hair behind her ear, and a shy smile played on her lips. Asa was working his charm, apparently. She was about to blush.

And I was jealous as hell.

If I could stop watching this, it would help. But I was punishing myself. Why, I wasn't sure. The universe had chosen to punish me by giving me life. That should be enough for any one person.

I wondered if Willa felt the same. Her mother hadn't wanted her for eleven years, and now she was back here, unwanted again. We had that in common. Children born to those who hadn't wanted us but kept us all the same. If anyone could understand me, it would be Willa. She'd be able to truly get what I was feeling. She'd felt similar.

But she deserved more. I was damaged. I'd never be good for her. It was time Willa had a chance at something better. Wishing I could be that didn't help either of us. I had to let it go.

People Make Mistakes

CHAPTER 35

WILLA

The entire lunch he'd watched me. Why? He was avoiding me like I was going to cling to him and demand marriage over a kiss. If he was so scared of getting near me and my suddenly turning into Crazy Girl, then why was he watching me? It was annoying. It messed with my head, and I was thinking agreeing to go to that dance tonight was a bad idea.

The blue dress I had worn to homecoming last year at my school hung on my closet door. So many memories went with that dress. They all had Poppy in them. We had fun that night. It was before the pot smoking had started and the drinking. Life had been safe then. Easy.

Why had we thought getting high was better? Why hadn't we stayed that way? We'd had fun back then. We had laughed and enjoyed life. But we'd let one guy into our world, and it had changed it all. Forever.

I wasn't sure I could wear that dress. Not again. I sank down onto the edge of my bed and stared at it. The desire to shove it back in my closet and curl up in bed was strong. I couldn't though. I'd said yes when Asa had asked me to the dance. I hadn't thought about it. I'd just said yes.

He was too nice for me to tell him no now. I liked him, and he seemed to like me. Then I had to go to this dance. But first I had to go to the game and watch him play. Lifting my eyes back up, I looked at the only dress I owned that was remotely appropriate. But I just couldn't wear it.

Sighing, I threw myself back on the bed and closed my eyes. I had three hours to get ready before Nonna would have to take me to the game. I wouldn't see Asa until afterward, seeing as they didn't go home on game day. He was with his team right now. My other option had been to ride with Ivy, and I'd opted out of that offer. She was nuts.

A knock on my bedroom door was brief before Nonna opened it on up. There were no locks on the interior doors of the house. There never had been. When I was younger, I hadn't cared. Now I liked my privacy, so it kinda sucked.

"You decide on what you're wearing?" she asked me.

I glanced back at the dress and frowned. "No."

Nonna followed my gaze, then walked into the room a little ways. "That the one you wore last year?"

Nodding, I looked away from it again. I hadn't been able to throw it out. Wearing it was too painful, but it was a memory of Poppy. I couldn't part with it.

"I've got a few of your mother's old dresses packed away. I might can alter them a little if you find one you want to wear."

I hadn't realized Nonna had kept anything of my mother's. They weren't very close. "How bad are they?"

Nonna smiled and shrugged. "Not bad. Fashion hasn't changed too much in the last sixteen years. You were one when she wore two of them."

That was probably my best option. I stood up and nodded. "Then let's go do this."

Not once in my life had I ever been inside my nonna's closet. I'd slept in her room as a child when I was scared, but I never got in her closet. She opened it up and motioned for me to come to her. "There's a couple in here that I think will fit just fine."

I wasn't so sure about this, but I was going to be open-minded. At least no one would have on the same circa-2001 dress. I walked over to her as she pushed her clothing aside and reached to the back of the closet near the wall.

The first dress she pulled out was a pink chiffon with a ballerina-type skirt. I was sure that was all the rage back in the day, but I wasn't feeling it. I crumpled my nose and shook my head. Nonna chuckled. "I wasn't a fan of it back then, either. But your mother had to have it."

If this was my mother's taste in high school, we weren't going to have success.

Next Nonna pulled out a cream baby-doll-style dress that was strapless and had an overlay of lace. It had a timeless look. Almost 1950s or earlier. I loved it. I reached for that one and held it up to me in front of the mirror. It fell a few inches above my knees. The only problem was I had no shoes for this.

"If you like that one, I have a pair of gold ballet flats your mother wore with it. She wore a seven then, like you."

"You still have them?" I asked, amazed.

Nonna nodded. "Yes. I thought one day you might need to use her things, so I kept them. Looks like I was right."

Again I wished that my nonna was my mother. She was a much better one than her daughter. I hadn't been a regret for Nonna. She had wanted and accepted me from the beginning. My mother made sure to remind me over and over that I had ruined her teen years.

"Thanks." I tried to mask the emotion in my voice. It

was a simple thing, keeping clothes I might need to borrow one day. But she had done it for me. That made it special. I didn't feel special often. Nonna had always been the one to give me that.

She smiled at me as she held out a shoe box. "Go on and get ready for your night. It's time you enjoyed yourself a little. Living in regret and guilt ain't healthy."

Nonna hadn't asked me the details of that night. She knew what my mother had told her, but not once had she asked me. I wanted to tell her my truth. My side of the story. It wasn't much better than what my mother had told, but it was the real story.

"I didn't know Quinn was there. Poppy's little sister," I started, and waited to see if she'd tell me to be quiet like my mother and stepfather had when I'd tried to explain. When she remained silent, I continued. "When I got there, I thought it was just us. We had friends coming over, and we were planning the party. We had been all week. Poppy's parents had left Quinn upstairs in bed asleep and told Poppy to watch her. Poppy didn't tell me. She didn't tell anyone Quinn was there. I think she thought everyone would leave if there was a kid there. I'm still not sure why. . . . I know she never imagined Quinn would get out of bed and go outside. Quinn was such a deep sleeper."

I paused and waited, but Nonna didn't say anything. "I

shouldn't have been smoking and drinking. I knew that, but I'd grown to enjoy the escape. All my worries and issues at home went away, and I enjoyed myself. But if I'd known Quinn was there, I'd have never done it. We always took care of Quinn when she was home. Never did any of that stuff when we were supposed to be watching her. I often wonder if Poppy had already been high when her parents left her with Quinn. That's the only thing that comes close to making sense."

Poppy loved her little sister. Quinn could be a pain sometimes, but Poppy protected her. We both did. I'd been so confused when I'd run outside to see Quinn's body floating in the pool. Why was she there? Where had she come from?

Poppy hadn't stopped screaming. Not when the ambulance arrived or the cops came. They had to sedate her to calm her down. Three days she was sedated because while awake all she did was scream and cry Quinn's name. It was the fourth day, when she had woken up alone, that she'd gone to her father's closet and found his pistol, then took her life.

"Tragedy strikes us all at one point in our life. People make mistakes, and some are lucky enough to walk away without lasting marks, while others live a lifetime with the choice they made. Can't change the past, Willa. But you can help others not make the same mistake." Nonna trusted me. She believed in me again. My heart felt full as I saw the love in her eyes. I hadn't felt loved in a very long time.

I thought about that the entire time I was getting dressed. I wanted a way to make Quinn's and Poppy's lives worthwhile. Make their marks on this world important and remembered. Thanks to Nonna, I had an idea.

What Is She Wearing?

CHAPTER 36

BRADY

I had been right. We had tightened the left side, and no one had made it through. Same play had ended in three touchdowns in the first half. We managed to use it and score one more touchdown in the second half. Then we'd had to switch things up a bit because the Trojans were catching on. In the end we won 38 to 17. Not a bad homecoming score. Could have been better.

Ivy was talking to the other girls standing around about her dress and where she had gotten it. I'd heard this story about ten times now. It was grating on my nerves. Did they seriously give a crap?

My attention moved to the entrance as Gunner came in with Serena, who was dressed like she was about to go dance on a pole. I was sure that made Gunner happy. I wished Ivy was dressed like she was about to hit a pole. At least I'd be interested in what she was saying. No, that was shallow. Damn, I needed to work on my thoughts. My momma had taught me better than that.

"What is she wearing?" Ivy's fake whisper was more of a loud hiss. Rolling my eyes, I mumbled an "I'll be back." Then I headed over to talk to West. Maggie was with him, but she looked about as excited to be here as I was. Although, she'd spent a good two hours getting ready, according to Mom. I'd talked to her after the game, and she'd wanted to tell me to make sure Maggie had a good time. She seemed to forget that my cousin was no longer my responsibility at these functions. She was dating West, who took good care of her. I was off the hook.

"Hey," West said with a nod. "Bottom of the third, that pass was a beauty."

I shrugged. "All my passes are beauties." That wasn't true and we both knew it, but we'd won, so it was time to smack talk. There were plenty of plays tonight I was disgusted with, but I'd deal with that later.

West chuckled. "You running off from Ivy already?"

I glanced back over my shoulder to see if Ivy was

headed my way, but my gaze never made it to her. Instead I was instantly locked on someone else.

Willa.

"Oh wow, I love her dress," Maggie said behind me.

Willa's blond hair was curled and hung loosely around her shoulders. Her eyes looked even bigger with the makeup she'd worn. The red lipstick on her mouth looked elegant with the pretty dress she was wearing.

"Asa was pumped about this date. Looks like he's happy," West added to the conversation that I was no longer having with them. My attention was completely on Willa. I took in every detail and wished like hell I'd broken this date with Ivy. I could have had Willa by my side tonight. But bringing myself to hurt Ivy hadn't been possible. She didn't deserve it.

I finally went back to her face, hoping to catch her eye, but her focus was elsewhere. I followed her gaze directly to Gunner, who was also watching her. It seemed as if the two of them were unaware of anyone else in the room. The reality of this was sinking in, and I wished it wasn't. If they wanted each other, why were they avoiding each other? And when the hell had this happened? I had been the one to kiss Willa. I had been the one to flirt with her. Gunner treated her like one of the guys. But maybe that was the difference.

I turned back around, unable to watch them any longer. If that was what I thought it was, then Gunner was a bigger dumbass than me. He'd brought Serena to this dance for a sure thing. When it looked like he could have had Willa.

Chances were after tonight that Willa wouldn't look at him the same way again. He had passed her off on me all week, and now he was at a dance with a girl dressed like a stripper. Smart.

Asa was my friend, but Willa was mine first. He'd have to just understand. I wasn't letting my guilt issues with breaking things off with Ivy stop me anymore. She'd already ruined my last homecoming dance.

I Don't Think He Has an Uncle

CHAPTER 37

WILLA

Comparing myself to someone else was never my thing. I was different in my own right, and I liked it. Now that I was comparing myself to Serena, part of me was ashamed of myself. The other part was giving in and measuring myself up against her. Problem was I was losing. Bad.

The skintight red dress she had on was so short, if she bent over you'd see her panties. I'd like to say she looked trashy, but she was every seventeen-year-old boy's dream date.

My dress no longer seemed so great. It took all my willpower to look away from the stunning couple they made. But I did it. I was here with Asa, who wanted my company. Gunner obviously did not. Fine.

"Want a drink?" Asa asked, glancing at me almost nervously.

"Sure."

"There's West and Maggie." He nodded in their direction. Brady was also with them. His back was to me, but even still, I liked the dark slacks he was wearing with the white oxford shirt. He wore it well.

Pointing out where West and Maggie were meant that was where we were headed, I soon realized.

Just before we reached them, there was a crash near the entrance, and everyone went silent as their attention was directed toward it. I stopped and turned like the rest of the room.

"Where's my motherfucking uncle!" a guy yelled at the top of his lungs. He slurred his words and stumbled, further knocking over tables and decorations as he went. "I know he's here!" The guy continued pointing as he turned in a half circle, squinting his eyes to focus.

"Shit," Asa muttered.

I almost asked him who that was when I saw Gunner step in front of him and grab his upper arm. It all fell into place then. That was Rhett Lawton, Gunner's brother. I hardly recognized him from six years ago. He looked more like a man now. He was calling Gunner his uncle to out him in public. The dirty secret the Lawtons were keeping was something Gunner wanted to remain a secret. Rhett should too, but it didn't look like he wanted to.

"I don't think he has an uncle," Asa whispered. "Dude must be hammered or stoned."

"I've got to go," I said by way of explanation as I hurried toward the exit Gunner was pushing Rhett through while he railed on and on loudly about his uncle.

I think Asa called out "Wait," but I ignored him. I had to help Gunner.

Rhett was taunting him when I reached them, asking for an allowance.

"Shut the fuck up," Gunner growled at him, completely frustrated.

I opened the door and met Gunner's gaze. No words were needed. He understood I was there to help. He reached into his pocket and pulled out his truck keys. "Go get my truck. It's parked in the left parking lot near the sign."

He threw me the keys; I caught them and nodded.

"Who's she? Are you dating my uncle? He's fucking loaded."

"Jesus, Rhett, shut up!" Gunner ordered, jerking his brother hard until he was far enough away from the door that his voice wasn't carrying inside.

"Everything okay?" Brady's voice stopped me as I turned to go get the truck.

"Yeah, peachy fucking great. Can't you tell?" Gunner snarled in response.

Brady shifted his gaze to me. "You leaving?"

"Going to get Gunner's truck."

He held out his hand. "Give me the keys. I'll go get it."

I looked to Gunner for direction and he nodded. He probably wanted Brady away from Rhett's mouth. So I tossed him the keys and gave him the directions that Gunner had given me.

Once Brady was out of earshot, Gunner sighed. "What the hell are you doing, Rhett?"

Rhett jerked free of Gunner and threw his hands up in the air. "I'm coming to see the crown bastard prince! What does it look like?"

Gunner winced, and I wanted to go slap my hand over his brother's mouth. Asshole.

"I'm taking you home," Gunner said as he glanced back at the door to make sure no one else had followed us out.

"Do I still get to live there?" Rhett asked in his drunken sarcastic tone.

Gunner ignored him and turned his attention to me. "Will you go make my excuses? I can't go back in there."

"Yes," I replied just as the door opened and out walked Asa, Serena, and Ivy, all looking for their dates.

"Shit," Gunner muttered.

"I got this," I assured him, and hurried toward them.

Ivy was surveying the area for Brady. Serena was glaring at me, and Asa looked concerned. "Brady has gone to get Gunner's truck so he can take Rhett home. He's had a little too much to drink. Why don't we all go back inside and let them deal with Rhett."

"I'm not taking orders from you. I don't even know you," Serena snapped in a haughty tone.

"Go inside, Serena. She's helping me. Jesus you're a bitch." Gunner raised his voice enough that Serena snapped her head back as if he'd slapped her.

"Fuck off, Gunner" was her response before she turned and strutted away.

"Are you going to need Brady to help you get him home?" Ivy's question was more of a whine.

"No," he snapped, and she beamed as if this was the best news she'd heard all day and went back inside.

I walked over to Asa. "They're good now," I told him.

He nodded, and we started to walk inside when Gunner's voice stopped me.

"Stay with me." His eyes were pained and lost. He needed me and that meant something.

Staying with him meant standing up my date. But could I tell him no when I was the only friend he had who knew the truth? Absolutely not. I also couldn't tell him no when

I knew he wanted me with him. The smart thing for me to do would be to stay with Asa. Be a normal teenager and focus on my goals. The reason I came back here.

That didn't matter. Gunner had become more important to me than all of that. Facing that now was the only thing I could do.

I looked up at Asa. "I have to stay with him."

Asa glanced at Gunner, then back at me, before he nodded and walked inside. He was disappointed. I'd seen it in his eyes.

Gunner's problems were bigger than losing your date to the dance.

Get in the Truck, Rhett

CHAPTER 38

GUNNER

Seven times I'd called his sorry ass. Not once had he answered or returned my call. Yet he shows up at the homecoming dance to yell shit about me being his uncle like a lunatic.

"There's Brady," Willa said, coming up to stand behind me. I should have let her go back inside with Asa, but I had needed her. Having her close helped. She knew the truth, and she was there as my center. Tonight wasn't going to get easier, and I didn't want to face it alone. I needed Willa with me. Having Willa there meant I could face anything. She calmed me and reassured me just being close. In my life there had never been someone like Willa. I think I knew that as a child. She was special. The kind of special you only get once.

After I'd avoided her for days, she had every right to ignore me and go back inside. But she'd stayed. She'd chosen me over Asa. Over that stupid dance in there. Willa made me feel like I had somewhere I belonged. Once Rhett had, because even though my parents weren't that fond of me, he'd loved me.

Now having my older brother, who used to fight my battles, throw me out there like he had tonight hurt. Willa made it hurt less. She eased it. Even before Brady had gotten out here, she had been helping me. She hadn't stood and stared at the scene.

"Thanks," I told her.

"Anytime" was her response. She was there. Again, something I'd never had before.

Brady pulled the truck up beside us. I started to give Brady an excuse to get him to go back inside when Willa walked over to him.

"Ivy is causing a scene. I told her you'd be right back. Go ease that over, and I'll help here. Ivy won't listen to me."

Brady turned his gaze to me as if he wasn't sure he should leave me alone.

"Go on. She's right. Crazy bitch came out here yelling and shit."

Brady nodded. "Okay, sorry about that. I'll be back in a few to see if you need me."

"Thanks," I said, knowing I'd be gone before he got back out here.

The doors opened again, and this time West, Nash, and Ryker all stepped outside. Shit, the whole crew was coming to help. "Help with that," I whispered to Brady, and he gave me an understanding nod.

"Get in the truck," I said in a lower voice to Rhett, and started moving him closer to the passenger door Willa had opened for me.

Rhett bumped into Willa, and I jerked him back. "Watch out!"

Rhett started cackling with manic laughter. "You like her. That's so sweet. Did you know he was my uncle? He's a bastard, but he's loaded."

I started to yell at him again, but Willa spoke first.

"Yes, I know, and from the looks of things, you pissing him off is stupid. Get ahold of yourself and don't make him your enemy. You need an allowance."

Rhett's eyes went wide, and for the first time all damn day I laughed.

"Who the fuck are you?" he asked, slurring his words more and more.

"I'm Willa Ames, you idiot," she retorted.

Then he smiled. "Willa Ames all grown up."

I knew that smile. He might be drunk, but he was attracted to her. Who wouldn't be? Willa was beautiful. And she was putting up with my drunk brother for me. I had been her choice when she'd been given one, and it made me feel deeper for her than I'd ever felt.

"Get in the truck, Rhett," I demanded, pushing him toward the now-open passenger side.

"Wait . . . I thought you moved away." He was still stuck on Willa.

"I moved back." The way she gave him annoyed, short responses was funny.

He gave her a flirty smile that he even pulled off well when he was drunk. "I might need to stay around town a little longer."

"You might not have a home to stay in if you don't get your drunk ass in my truck now," I added with more force, and shoved him until he stumbled and had to grab the seat to keep from falling.

"Yes sir, Uncle, sir. You sure got real bossy with all this power."

I glanced at Willa, who rolled her eyes at his comment. I

needed that little touch of humor right now. She was keeping me from losing my shit. I owed her.

When Rhett finally climbed up in my truck, I wanted to ask Willa to get in too. I wanted her with me. I didn't want to ask her to miss the entire night, but going back to that house with Rhett like this sounded terrifying.

But could I bring her into this shit? Was that even fair?

No.

Before I could even say anything, she opened the back door on my extended cab and climbed inside. She didn't ask me or wait to be invited. She was just going. My chest felt full. It was an odd sensation I wasn't accustomed to.

I wanted to say thanks again, but I couldn't at the moment. My tight chest was making my throat feel weird. So I climbed into the driver's seat and got us away from the school parking lot before Rhett did something else stupid.

"We going to your castle?" he asked as he laid his head back on the seat.

"What's your deal? Do you think I want this? That being our grandfather's bastard is a good thing? Jesus, Rhett, stop focusing on how this affects you."

He laughed again, and I really wanted to stop and push him out, then take Willa somewhere alone so I could kiss her again. This time I wasn't running.

"Isn't everything always about you?" Rhett snarled.

I had no idea what that meant. I shot him a glare and turned onto the road that led to our house.

"Every time I wanted something, Mother always said no if you couldn't have the same. So Dad didn't get it. I missed out on all kinds of shit because of you. Now I know why. The damn money was all yours."

Gripping the steering wheel tighter, I slammed on the breaks and threw the truck in park.

"My entire life I've spent trying to please a man who would never accept me. A man I thought was my father. I was a kid, Rhett, and I wanted my father to love me as much as he loved his other son. Nothing I did was enough. It was cruel. I get it now. It's unfair but I get it. But don't dare give me your sob story over some bullshit you wanted and didn't get because of me. You were given what I never got. Our parents love."

"They aren't our parents. We only share a mom."

Those words would change our relationship forever. I didn't care that he was drunk. I didn't care that he was bummed that the fortune he thought was all his wasn't. The coldness in his tone took something from me. Something that I'd never get back.

"Then he's lucky. I'd hate to know he had a chance of turning out like you," Willa said from the backseat.

I glanced up at her in the rearview mirror. I had someone on my side. I didn't deserve her, but I was thankful I had her.

I Was Messed Up for Life

CHAPTER 39

WILLA

When I jumped in the back of the truck, I hadn't thought through what I would do when we got to Gunner's house. If I went inside to the middle of this firestorm, then Nonna would be furious. I couldn't upset her; she was all I had.

Sending Gunner inside to face this alone seemed impossible too. As we passed the driveway to Nonna's house and he didn't pull in, I knew he was expecting me to go with him to face this mess.

I guess maybe he'd let me live in the tree house if Nonna kicked me out. That was a joke, but still. I might need lodging soon.

Gunner parked in front of his house and turned to Rhett. "Get out," he ordered, but he didn't move.

We were doing a drop off. This was much better. I'd get in no trouble for this. Rhett muttered a few curse words, then opened the door to stumble out. "Where's my car?" he asked, looking around.

"At the school. You're too drunk to drive. Get it in the morning." Gunner then turned to look at me. "You want to get up here?"

I unbuckled and climbed over the seat, then closed the door that Rhett had left open. "Are we going back to the dance?" I asked, confused.

Gunner shook his head. "Naw, I can't deal with that right now. You okay with going somewhere else?"

I was okay with whatever. Gunner needed me, and I enjoyed being with him. I had him back. Being ignored by him the past few days had been hard.

"Sure," I replied, then felt a twinge of guilt over Asa. I had run off on him. I probably should go back, but something kept me here.

"I wish I could just leave this town and not look back. No parents, no last name, no fucking anything. Just run. You know?"

I understood why he wanted to now, but that wouldn't be forever. He hadn't had time to let it all sink in yet.

Adjusting to all this was just the beginning for him.

"You did good tonight, dealing with Rhett. If I didn't know better, I'd have thought you were the oldest."

Gunner grinned and glanced over at me. "Thanks. That was a first. Normally it's Rhett getting my ass out of situations. Not me being the levelheaded one about things."

I didn't remember much about Rhett other than he was a spoiled elitist back then. I hadn't known how to describe him when I was a kid, but looking back, I got why I hadn't cared for him much.

"After the way he's acted the past week, I wonder if Riley *hadn't* been full of shit," Gunner said, more to himself than to me. I wasn't sure what he was talking about. But I perked up at the mention of Riley's name.

"Did he and Riley date?" I asked, wondering why she had warned me against them and why she seemed to be hated around here.

"No. Me and Riley dated. Until she blamed Rhett for raping her and getting her pregnant."

Oh. Wow. Not what I had expected to hear.

"We hadn't even had sex. She was scared of it, and we were younger. Then she starts saying Rhett raped her and she was pregnant. My parents, or rather Rhett's parents, made it go away. And her. But still it hung in the air around here for a while. Almost cost Rhett his scholarship. She admitted she'd lied, then left town."

The girl I'd met didn't seem the type to lie about something like that, but then I'd barely spent any time with her. Rhett, on the other hand, might just do that. "She came back, didn't she?"

Gunner shrugged. "Yeah, I guess. I don't know. She gave you a ride, so I guess I'm lucky there. I wouldn't have wanted you walking on that dark road for miles."

Sounded like she had a sordid past much like my own. I hadn't seen her since that night. From all the girls in this town I'd met so far, I thought Riley would be the one I would bond with the best.

Poppy's face immediately settled itself firmly in my head, and I squashed that thought. I had a best friend once, and I'd not been there when she needed me. I hadn't saved her or Quinn. I didn't need another friend like Poppy. I wasn't good at that.

"Where are we going?" I asked, wanting to change the subject.

"To the lake," he responded.

The lake that I remembered was off limits to us as kids. It was far out on the opposite side of the Lawton property from Nonna's. Nonna's house sat at one back corner. The lake sat at the other. Apparently Gunner's "father" had had a younger sister when they were kids who drowned back there after getting bit by a snake.

"I've heard about the lake but never actually seen it," I said, suddenly curious.

Gunner shrugged. "Not that grand. But it does have a waterfall that my grandfather . . . or father . . . whoever the hell he is, put there in memory of my aunt Violet. Or I guess she was my sister. Fuck." He ended with a mutter.

"When did you first go back there?" I asked, hoping to get his mind from going in the direction it was currently headed.

"When I was twelve. Nash, Brady, West, and me all decided to go camp down there. Didn't end well when my parents found us. My mom cried and cried. I was surprised she cared so much. That was the first time in my life I actually felt like she loved me. Guess that's why I still come here."

He pulled off the main drive that circled the Lawton residence, and we went down a grassy path that had been taken before. I was sure by him. The moon was almost full, and it made the water up ahead sparkle. I wondered about the girl who had drowned here and how old she'd been. Had she meant to sneak off to swim that day, or had someone brought her here? The little girl who never got to grow up and experience life always intrigued me. But Gunner never had these answers, and he was too afraid to ask. We had talked about it when we were younger and wondered what her story was.

"It's beautiful out here. Peaceful." I didn't know Gunner's real father. He had passed away when Gunner was young, but if he'd memorialized his daughter this way, I thought he must have been a nice man. Not like his older son, who I'd never seen say a kind word.

"It's my place to escape. They don't know I come here, and even if they do, they don't care anymore. I guess me drowning would be helpful. They'd get to keep all that Lawton money and power to themselves. Not hand it over to the bastard son."

His words were so raw as he spoke them it made my heart hurt. Even now, the cocky full-of-himself teenage boy still felt unwanted. Unloved. I hated that for him. Gunner was special. He wasn't all he flashed around. He was damaged, but deep down he was kind. He cared. He was just too scared to show anyone.

"Brady and West would be devastated if you drowned. So would the other guys. They love you. Nonna would be a mess. She's always loved you. . . . And I'd be devastated too." I wanted him to remember it wasn't just family that mattered. He had friends around him who cared. He wasn't alone and unwanted.

He turned his head so his eyes locked with mine.

"You'd be devastated?" he asked. A very small upward turn on the corner of his lips made me smile. I was also blushing and that was silly, but I couldn't help it.

"Yes. Of course."

He glanced down at my hand, and then reached over with his and slipped it over mine. "I shouldn't have run after the kiss," he said, still staring down at our hands. "It just . . . was more than I expected. And . . ." He lifted his eyes to meet mine. "It scared the hell out of me. Never felt that before."

The butterflies that Brady had once given me didn't compare to the bats currently going off in my stomach as Gunner lifted his head and his gaze met mine again. Tonight I'd come to help him. Be his friend. I wasn't ever going to do the girl thing and demand he respond to me or explain. He had bigger issues than a kiss right now.

So the fact he was explaining, and the reason why he had run, meant something. It meant something big, and that terrified me. Because I was also taught already that I wasn't lovable and love hurts. I didn't want to love Gunner Lawson. Not in a way he could break me. I was too broken already.

"When shit went down tonight with Rhett, I felt so fucking alone. Then there you were. The first one to me.

The first one ready to help. And in that moment I knew. That kiss had shaken me because you were it. The it I didn't want. The it I'd been so sure would never come my way because I didn't intend to look for it." He paused, then smiled and shook his head. "My brother was yelling drunken shit and I was supposed to be shutting him up, but in that moment all I could think was 'I get it. Why people fall in love. I so fucking get it.'"

Tears stung my eyes, and I was thankful for the limited lighting out here. I didn't want his words to affect me like this, but that wasn't my choice. They were burrowing inside me and latching on. Making me want things I didn't deserve nor could I have.

"I'll always be here for you," I told him, unable to say the other things I was thinking.

"I want more than that. I want you. I want to be able to kiss you anytime I want. I want to hold your hand in the halls. Hell, I want to be made fun of by the guys for wanting to be near you all the time." He laughed at his words, and my heart squeezed so tight I had a hard time catching my breath.

This was moving at a pace I hadn't expected. Although I wanted it too, I had to be fair. He had to know my past. All of it. And understand that I was messed up for life. Yet want all these things with me anyway.

My Plans for the Future
Had Just Taken a Massive Turn

CHAPTER 40

GUNNER

"I didn't tell you everything. The whole story. About why Poppy took her life." Willa said those words as if they were being torn from her body and she wanted to grab them and pull them back.

I had just told her I was in love with her without actually saying the words, and she was wanting to tell me why her friend killed herself. I didn't understand this, so I remained quiet and waited. It was something she needed to say, and I would do whatever she needed me to do.

"We were drunk . . . and high. But we were at Poppy's house and that was safe. We thought. Staying home while her parents worked at their restaurant, we had friends over and partied there. No one drove. It was safe. We weren't out causing trouble. I liked it. The escape it gave me. I wanted to forget that my mother tolerated me, but she and her husband both would have preferred not to have me around. I was the extra child. The one they didn't want. But she was stuck with. So the weed and the vodka were my happy place. I didn't care about anything when I was doing either or both." She paused and twisted her hands tightly in her lap before staring outside as if she were there again. At the house. Seeing it all happen in front of her.

"Everyone makes mistakes," I assured her, because, seriously, if she was beating herself up over getting drunk and high, that was a touch overboard.

She nodded. "They do. But some don't walk away from it. We didn't. Not Poppy, not me, and not Quinn."

Who? "Was Quinn another friend?"

"Quinn was three years old. She was Poppy's little sister. I loved her smile and her laugh. She was always happy, and she loved me. That night . . . she'd been upstairs in her bed asleep. I hadn't known. Poppy didn't mention it, and normally she would say we had Quinn to watch. We didn't drink or smoke when we had Quinn there. But that night . . . Poppy had thought it would be safe. Quinn was in bed, so she didn't tell me. I had no idea. No one did. Until . . ." She paused again, and a sick knot formed in my stomach. I wasn't being a pussy, but, dammit, if this story was going where I thought it was, Willa had a lot more that darkened her eyes than I had first assumed.

"I was lying on the floor after looking for cheese balls in the pantry. I had the munchies. I'd been too drunk to stand up. Then the scream . . . it was so full of pain, terror, and agony, I'll never forget it. Poppy was screaming, and I scrambled up and ran outside toward her voice. I knew something was wrong, but I hadn't been prepared to see Quinn floating in the pool, facedown and lifeless. I'll—" She stopped and swallowed as a silent tear ran down her face. "I'll never forgive myself. I'll never forget. And Quinn will never have a chance at life. Neither will Poppy. Four days later Poppy took her life. She couldn't live with knowing Quinn was dead because we hadn't been watching her. She blamed herself completely. I should have asked. I should have checked, but I didn't. It wasn't all her fault. When the paramedics came, so did the police. We were all arrested for intoxication, drug use, and possession, and then there was Quinn's death. It was never proven to be murder because it wasn't. But we had been left to babysit, and she'd drowned due to our drug and alcohol use. I spent the next six months after Poppy and

Quinn's funeral in a correctional center for girls. When I got out, my bags were packed and at the front door of my mother's house. I had no one to call but Nonna. She bought me a bus ticket and brought me back here."

Fuck.

Double Fuck.

How did I respond to that? Jesus, she'd been through hell over one night of partying. I'd partied many times with no repercussions other than a bad hangover. Her whole world had been tossed.

"I'll never be able to forgive myself. For Quinn or Poppy. I don't expect anyone else to."

"Willa, nothing was your fault. We're teenagers. We are allowed to make mistakes—it's part of growing up. What happened to you isn't fair. You didn't know the little girl was there. How is her death your fault? It isn't. Neither is Poppy's. Poppy was at fault. She should have kept her head clear and watched over her sister. She couldn't live with the fact she let her sister down. But not one part of this was your fault. You were a casualty."

I believed every word I said, but Willa didn't. It was in her eyes as she turned to look at me finally. She'd kept her focus on the lake while she spoke. "I should have asked. They left Quinn home often. I should have asked."

"Quinn wasn't your responsibility."

She didn't say anything as she lifted a hand to catch a new tear that had broken loose. "April the fifteenth was the night Quinn drowned. On March fifteenth she'd turned three years old. We had celebrated with a Sofia the First birthday party. Purple princess stuff everywhere."

I didn't have a clue who Sofia the First was, but she needed to talk about this. I had a feeling she hadn't talked about it one time since it happened. All I could do for her was listen.

"She had dark brown curls like Sofia the First, and I always called her Princess Sofia to make her giggle. I'd pretend I got confused and thought she was the real Sofia the First. She'd say, 'I'm Quinn, silly. Remember me?' and I'd act surprised. That only made her laugh harder. They were my home. Quinn and Poppy. They wanted me there. I was accepted there . . . I miss them."

If I could have one wish in this world, it would be to go back in time and fix this for her. To right this so she didn't have to feel guilt over it her entire life. I didn't care about my family shit. So I was a rich kid whose momma got knocked up by the man who was supposed to be my grandfather. Not a big deal when you're dealing with death. Willa had so much more darkness to overcome, and I would be there for her no matter what. She could try and push me away, but I wasn't going.

I was in love with Willa Ames. The girl she had once been and the woman she was becoming. Her heart was so damn big and accepting. Just being near her made things seem better.

My plans for the future had just taken a massive turn.

You're Special, Willa Ames

CHAPTER 41

WILLA

I had to stop myself from saying more. It was like the flood gates had opened, and I couldn't stop the words from pouring out of my mouth. All the stuff I'd kept to myself. The memories only I had now. I needed to say them. I needed someone else to know about Quinn's smile and her giggle. It was like I in some way could give her life again. Just remembering.

"Were you there when Quinn was born?" His question surprised me. I hadn't been expecting him to speak at all. I was reminiscing about a dead little girl he didn't know. But he seemed to truly care.

"Yes. My mom let me go to the hospital with Poppy's

dad and her. We sat in the waiting room for hours reading books, eating snacks, and looking through the large window at all the other babies that came in to the nursery. It was a fun day. When Quinn was brought into the nursery in their dad's arms, he had the biggest smile. Poppy hugged me, and we laughed and clapped at the little baby with dark curls already on her head. We were sure there had never been another baby that adorable."

"So she was like your sister too." He wasn't asking a question. It was a statement. And he was right. She'd been my little sister just like Poppy's. I had never missed a birthday or Halloween taking her trick-or-treating. All my good memories had Quinn and Poppy in them. It was funny how my most painful did as well.

"They both were. My sisters. Losing them took part of me. The best part."

It was true. When they had laid them both in the ground, I had felt my heart go with them. My joy, my happiness, all of the good things went too. I couldn't accept those with someone else.

"They would want you to find happiness again. To live for them. They won't get life, and because of that you need to live it for them. Not forgiving yourself and placing blame on yourself isn't doing their lives justice. They'd want more for you. This would be disappointing to them, Willa. They don't blame you, and you shouldn't either. You want to remember them, then do it. Talk about them. I'll listen. Tell me everything. I'm here. But don't live a life with no hope for happiness, because it isn't fair to their memory."

I turned to look at him. Had those words just come out of Gunner Lawton's mouth? Where had the fun-loving playboy gone? I knew he was deeper than he let the world see, but I hadn't been prepared for that. And if he meant them as much as it sounded like he did, then was he right? Was I not doing justice to their memory?

"Do you believe what you just said?" I asked him.

He nodded. "Hell yeah I do. Every damn word. And if you don't listen now, be ready to hear them over and over again, because I intend to tell you until you get it. Until they're real to you, too. You're special, Willa Ames. You always were. They loved you because they saw in you what I did that day I caught you playing with my army men. Neither of those girls would want to think you gave up on life to punish yourself over their deaths. Neither was your fault, and deep down you know that. You just can't say the truth because it hurts too much. You loved Poppy too much. But it was her fault, Willa. It was Poppy's fault, and she knew it. She couldn't live with it. That is the truth. Accept it."

The tears I'd been fighting off, or at least trying to by

only letting a few free at a time, began to stream down my face. Sobs that racked my body broke free, and I bent forward, wrapping my arms around my stomach to keep from completely falling apart.

He was right.

But that hurt so much.

Two strong arms wrapped around me, and I went willingly into his embrace. He didn't say anything more, and even if he had, I wouldn't have been able to hear him over the sobbing. The pain I'd bottled up for so long I let free. I accepted the truth. The one no one had told me until now. The one I was afraid to believe or accept because I didn't want to blame Poppy. I loved her.

But to move on in life I had needed to hear it. Gunner had given me what no one else ever had. Reassurance that I deserved to live too. So many times I'd thought I should have killed myself. I loved Quinn, so why was I able to live and Poppy hadn't been? Had I loved her less? Was I selfish? I had asked myself so many questions and battled with my own emotions over this for so long I forgot the basic facts. The ones that tonight I'd finally said out loud. To someone who was willing to listen.

I cried in his arms for what felt like an eternity. The front of his shirt was soaked with my tears, but his arms never loosened. In fact his hold got tighter the longer we stayed there. When it all started to dry up and the heaviness that I'd carried for so long began to ease, giving me my first real deep breath in months, I lifted my head and stared up at him. This boy who I never expected to be my hero. I never guessed would hold me when I fell apart. This boy who had been by my side through many of my life's changes. Maybe it had always been, but I hadn't known it or understood it. But I knew it now.

I loved Gunner Lawson.

"Thank you." My voice cracked as I said the words.

He pressed a kiss to my forehead. "I'm always here."

Yes, he was. Even though his life was shit, he was still here listening to me. "I soaked your shirt."

He gave me a small grin. "It'll wash up just fine."

"I . . . I haven't talked about that or really cried like that about it."

Gunner pulled me closer to him. "I'm glad you did with me. You needed it. You've beat yourself up enough. You need to heal, Willa. You need to move on."

"I can't ever forget them."

He shook his head. "No. You can't. You need to live for them and remember them while you're living the life they didn't get. Do it for them. Do it for you."

"I love you, Gunner." The words were out of my mouth before I could stop them.

I hadn't thought through how he would react or what he would say, because I honestly hadn't meant to say it out loud. But I had said it. Now I had to own it and deal with the repercussions.

Which ended up being nothing. Without a word he kissed my forehead again, then took me home.

It Wasn't Like We Were the Trumps

CHAPTER 42

GUNNER

Knowing you love someone and saying it out loud are two completely different things. The first is startling, and the second is terrifying. I accepted the fact I loved Willa even though I'd sworn to never love anyone. She'd broken through my walls, and I was glad. She made me happy. Being with her was as complete as I'd ever felt.

The bravery it was going to take in order to tell her that, though, I was afraid I lacked greatly. I wasn't even having to face the fact she may not feel the same way. There was no laying it out there to be shot down. She'd already said the words to me. But even still, saying them made them real. As real as love could be for me. I'd never told anyone I loved them.

Not even my parents. Because they'd never once told me. I hadn't been raised in a house where the word love was spoken easily, like Brady and West. It hadn't been spoken at all within the Lawton walls.

When she'd said the words so easily, my chest constricted because it was the first time I'd heard them. I hadn't been able to say anything in return. Hell, I almost said thank you. It was a gift many take for granted that others have never been given.

In that moment I didn't have the adequate words for what I was feeling. All I'd been able to do was hold her and kiss her head. Tears had stung my eyes, and the emotion had made it hard for me to say anything. She'd given me hope. I hadn't realized I had none until her.

If she had a cell phone, I'd at least be able to text her what I was feeling. But that wasn't possible, and she deserved more than a well-written text message. I had to man up and say it to her. Let her know I loved her.

At this moment though I had to walk into my house and face the shit waiting on me there. Hopefully, Rhett was passed out drunk. I opened the back door and headed for the stairs without listening for voices. If I could avoid them all, I would.

The silence was a relief as I rushed up the stairs and down the hall to the only sanctuary I had here, my room.

No one ever came in there but Ms. Ames to clean it. Everyone else left me alone. When I was younger, that made me lonely. Now it is the only way I can live here.

Slinging my door open, I stepped inside, only to freeze when my eyes landed on my mother sitting in the chair across from my bed. I couldn't remember a time in my life she'd ever been in this room. Seeing her here now was discomforting.

"Hello, Gunner," she said in a voice that didn't hold hostility or annoyance like it normally did when she said my name.

"Mom," I replied, not moving inside any more because my safe place had just become foreign to me.

"Come in and close the door. There are some things I need to tell you. It's time you know."

I was pretty damn sure I didn't want to know any more of her secrets. The last one was enough to last me a lifetime. "If you're about to tell me that Grandmother Lawton is my real mother or I'm the offspring of an aunt I don't know about, could you save it? I need some sleep." My tone was annoyed. Because I was fucking annoyed.

My mother frowned her disapproving cotillion frown she was so good at, and I pointed to the door. "I'm serious," I added.

She shook her head. "Stop acting like a child, Gunner.

It's time you grew up and became a man. This immature rebellious persona you're so fond of has to end now. You have an empire to control whether you like it or not."

I wouldn't call the Lawton money an empire, but my mother had always acted loftier than we were. Lawton, Alabama, was . . . well for one it was in Alabama. Jesus. It wasn't like we were the Trumps.

"I'm a senior in high school, not a college graduate. Your other son is in college, and his drunk ass came to the homecoming dance tonight yelling and calling me his uncle. It was a shining moment for the Lawton Empire," I mocked.

Her face tensed. She didn't like scenes, and Rhett had caused a major one. Maybe she should be in his room giving him a damn lecture on growing up. I wanted her to love me. Saying I didn't care was a lie. She was my mother, and I'd tried to make her happy. I'd just never been able to.

She shook her head as if that didn't matter. "Rhett isn't the Lawton heir. You are. It's different for you. And Rhett always expected that it would always be his one day. I think your father thought he'd win in the end. But the will is ironclad. Your grandfather made sure of it. This is all yours when you turn eighteen."

Eighteen? I'd be eighteen next month.

"You mean my father made sure it was ironclad. If we

are going to admit my paternity, then we at least need to claim it and stop acting like the dick you're married to is my father. I never wanted him for a father. The only good thing about this is he's not."

My mother frowned again. "The rest of the world needs to believe he is. It's the only way to save face."

"Whose? Yours?" I asked with a snarl. I didn't care about saving fucking face. It was Lawton.

"Yours too. Don't think for a moment that the truth wouldn't put a damper on your life. You'd be the Lawton bastard. Do you want that? A girl from a good family won't marry you with that taint in your past."

"Thank God for that. Never did much care for the cotillion bitches."

"Gunner! This is serious."

I nodded. "Yes, it is. You screwed around with your father-in-law and made a baby, then lied to that baby his entire life. It's pretty damn serious. Now I'd like to go to bed. It's been a long night. "

"I didn't screw around with him." Her voice had taken a hysterical tone. "He raped me!"

This shit just kept getting worse.

The Name Lawton Means Nothing

CHAPTER 43

WILLA

Turning in circles in the middle of a large open field I'd never seen before in my life, I couldn't enjoy the flowers and beauty surrounding me. Because there was this odd tapping noise that I couldn't find.

Tap, tap, tap.

Then a pause

Tap, tap, tap.

Pause.

The pattern was driving me crazy, and I wanted to yell at it to stop.

Then I woke up.

Tap, tap, tap.

There it was again, and this time I was in my bed and that noise was coming from my window. I threw the covers back, stepped out of bed, and walked over to the window to peek through the curtain. Either there was an animal out there annoying me, or someone was being polite before they broke into the house and murdered us all. Whichever it may be, I was checking it out.

Gunner wasn't who I expected. I had really been leaning toward a bird on the window. I unlocked the top and quietly slid it up.

"Hey," I whispered, wondering if I might still be asleep. If so, at least the tapping had stopped.

"Tree house," he whispered back, nodding his head in the direction of the tree house.

"Now?" I asked, confused. It had to be at least two in the morning.

"Please" was his simple response, but it was enough. Something was wrong.

"Let me put on a hoodie and some shoes."

He nodded, then tucked his hands in his pockets and waited.

If I got caught sneaking out with Gunner, I was done for. Nonna trusted me. I had that back. If she caught me, then I'd lose that trust. And I needed it. I needed her trust . . . her love. But for Gunner I would just about do anything. Another risk I was willing to take. He wouldn't have come here if he didn't need me.

I blindly reached in my closet, not wanting to turn on my lights and draw attention to myself. Nonna was a heavy sleeper, but she was across the hall. This house wasn't big. Feeling my way, I found a hoodie and a pair of flip-flops.

Gunner was still at the window waiting on me when I got both items on my body. My hair was probably a mess, but I didn't have time to worry about that. I doubted that was a concern of Gunner's anyway. This had to do with his brother, I was sure.

Slipping the window up as far as it would go, I threw one leg out and then ducked my head, maneuvering the rest of my body out until my other leg could follow. "I'll leave it open," I said as quietly as I could.

His hand slid over mine and squeezed it. Without any more words we walked out into the darkness toward the tree house. I tried to wait for him to say something, but when we were far enough away from Nonna's that we could safely talk, he still hadn't spoken.

So I did.

"What time is it?"

"About two thirty."

He had brought me home by eleven. That had been my

curfew. I'd known he was going back to face Rhett, if Rhett was even awake still.

"Things go bad with Rhett?" I asked.

He shrugged. "Not really. He was asleep when I got back."

Oh.

Then why was I sneaking out of the house?

"You okay?" I was trying to give him enough space to tell me exactly what was going on without prying.

"I am now."

That was nice. Really sweet actually. I liked it.

But I still wanted to know why I'd just snuck out.

He stood back and motioned for me to go up the tree house ladder first. So I did. Only because it was so dark out, he couldn't see my butt that well.

When we were both inside, I turned to ask him what this was about, and his hands circled my wrists and tugged my body against his. Then his mouth covered mine, and I didn't care anymore about sneaking out and what was wrong with Gunner. I just wanted this kiss. The softness of his lips. The smell of the soap he used rose from the skin on his neck. I couldn't get close enough.

His hands moved to my hips, and held me there as he tasted me as thoroughly as I was tasting him. There was no worry of him running this time. I would tackle him if he tried. I wasn't letting this go again.

It made all the cheesy romance movies I'd seen appear realistic. That one kiss that changes everything no longer seemed like a fantasy. It was real. I was experiencing it yet again.

When Gunner finally pulled back, I protested with what sounded like a whine. I was pathetic. I needed to control myself.

"Run away with me," he said, so close still his breath tickled my lips and nose.

I almost nodded and agreed with whatever he was saying when I realized what he was actually saying. I paused. I couldn't agree to that. We had high school to finish and college to go to. Running away wasn't in the plans.

"What are you talking about? We can't run away," I said logically even though that kiss still had my toes curled up in my flip-flops.

"I can't live here under this Lawton name. With a family who hates me for all that I represent to them. I'm proof of pain and destruction. I hate it. I want to just be me somewhere that the name Lawton means nothing.

"I can't leave. I'm on probation. This"—I held out my hands—"this is my last chance. I don't get another."

Gunner sighed in frustration. "I have enough money that we can run and they'll never find us. We can start a new life. Get new names. Be us without the bullshit of our pasts. Leave our demons here in Lawton and get the hell away from them. Forget it all happened."

He made it sound so easy, and I could see he believed it would be easy. That we could just start a new life. But either he was tired or he thought he had more power than he did. They'd find us. "It isn't that simple."

"It can be. Don't you trust me?"

I did trust him, but the way he was talking was crazy. "We can't just leave. They'd look for us, and we'd be running forever. Eventually they'd find us. Besides, I can't do that to Nonna. She's always been there for me. Always stood in the gap and never let me down. Leaving her without a word would be wrong. She'd worry herself sick."

Gunner paced back and forth, running his hands through his hair. He reminded me of a caged lion trying to claw his way to freedom. Something had set him off. He hadn't been manic when he'd brought me home.

"What happened? Why are you wanting to run away now?"

He threw his head back and laughed loudly. "Now? Hell, Willa, I've wanted to run away most of my life. I've never been wanted. Not once. Then the one person on earth to ever tell me they love me won't go with me. I guess I don't understand love that well, because I thought that meant you loved me enough to go with me."

That was a low blow. Throwing my words back in my face. Words that I had meant and still did. But using them like this was wrong.

"Because I love you doesn't mean I'm willing to hurt my nonna. And because I love you I won't let you hurt your future. You have college ahead of you. A lifetime to live somewhere else and be something other than a Lawton. But leaving now won't fix anything."

He stopped pacing and turned to look at me. "She was raped. My mother didn't have an affair with her father-in-law. He raped her, and then she tried to have an abortion. He threatened to ruin her name and toss her out if she killed me. So she had me to save herself. My real father then left it all to me in his will to basically say 'fuck you' to the rest of the family. He was sadistic and cruel, and I was his tool to punish them with. He hated my father because, like me, he was a bastard. My father isn't his child. I'm his only blood."

Oh God. My stomach twisted, and I sat down on the wooden bench behind me. How sick could the Lawtons get? Could this get worse? Just when I thought it was bad enough, it got more deranged.

"The mansion my grandmother lives in is mine. She's never said a kind word to me in my life. Yet she lives on my money. I want to donate the whole damn estate to children's cancer research and leave. Let this town forget there was a Lawton family that founded it. Because they are all crazy."

I understood being hurt by your family. I also understood not feeling loved by your family. However, I did have Nonna. He hadn't even had that. My heart broke for him. If I could run away with him, I would. But that wasn't going to fix anything. Running from your problems never worked. They wouldn't disappear, and they'd follow you. I'd tried that, and it hadn't been my cure. Facing it and dealing with it was how I learned to survive.

"We only have six months left of senior year. Then we leave this place. You can go and not look back. Donate all you want. Make your life outside of Lawton. But don't run. Face this and conquer it. I'm here, and I'm not going anywhere."

He sat on the bench across from me and dropped his head into his hands. "I hate that place. That house. I hate it."

"Nonna's sofa is always open."

He didn't say anything for a few moments, and we sat in silence. I let him get his emotions together. He was raw, and I wished I could go to his house and coldcock every person in there. But that would only get me back in a correctional center.

"Next month I turn eighteen. It'll all be mine then."

Wow. I hadn't realized it was so soon that it became his.

There was a lot of pressure riding on him now. It was just going to get worse.

"I'm kicking them all out. Starting with the man I've called Father all my life. I considered letting Mom stay, but she wanted to abort me. Not sure I can forgive that. She doesn't love or want me. Why should I love or want her? The little boy that once sought her affection is long gone."

"It's a fair decision," I agreed, but I wondered if it was really what would make him happy. Sometimes the revenge we seek doesn't meet our expectations. It only hurts us.

"Marry me—move in with me," Gunner said in that insane tone again he'd used when he had asked me to run away.

"Marry you? Gunner we are seventeen. We can't marry." He needed to go to bed. He was getting delirious.

"I'm a multimillionaire. We can do whatever the fuck I want."

This wasn't what he really wanted. Right now he wanted to act out and hurt his family because all they'd done was hurt him. I wasn't going to help him with his plotting. I loved him. It was real. Not a toy or a game.

Standing up, I knew I had to leave. He needed to go home and get some sleep, and I was about to act like a complete girl and cry. He was using my love as a tool like he was using his money. I didn't want to be a weapon to hurt anyone. That wasn't what love was about.

"Loving someone doesn't mean allowing them to use you for their benefit. It just means they have a place in your heart. A place that they earned. I'm going to leave now before you hurt me any more with words you don't mean. Good night, Gunner."

He didn't run after me. He let me go.

I ran toward the house as the tears welled up in my eyes. Loving Gunner Lawton would never be easy. I wasn't sure he could love me in return. Didn't matter. I loved him. I just couldn't bend to his demands. I didn't owe him anything. He needed to learn that it wasn't all about that.

With my mind on Gunner's words and tears blurring my vision, I didn't see Nonna standing on the front porch until it was too late.

Please Do, Father Dear

CHAPTER 44

GUNNER

Rhett's bedroom was next to mine. When we had been kids, we'd liked it. But this morning, when I had gotten practically no sleep, I hated it. Him slamming drawers and blaring music was to piss me off. He was acting like I'd done this. How did he figure this shit was my fault?

When something hit the wall between our rooms, I threw my covers back and jumped out of bed. The asshole wanted me awake. Well he had me awake. Storming out of my room, I headed for his and didn't bother to knock before opening his door and slamming something myself.

"What the fuck is your problem?" I roared.

Rhett was still in his pajama pants, and a basketball was

in is hands. Apparently he'd been tossing that at the wall. Real mature, dickhead.

"What? Can't I move around in my own room now? Or are there rules I don't know about to keep the king of the castle happy?"

"GOD! Would you listen to yourself? You sound like a ten-year-old with a jealousy issue. I did nothing to you, Rhett. Our mother and your grandfather slept together. I wasn't alive, but that created me. No way was that my fucking fault. So get a grip and stop acting like a cocksucker."

Rhett glared at me. I wasn't sure he'd ever looked at me with so much venom before. Not even when we were younger and actually fought about things. There was pure hatred in his eyes. Even knowing this wasn't anything I could control, he blamed me.

"Then don't accept it. Give it to Dad where it belongs. He's the oldest son. Not you. The inheritance should be his. The OLDEST son's." My chest hurt. Once he'd been someone I could rely on to keep me safe. To be on my side. That was all gone now. The greed had taken over.

So that was it. He was the oldest, and he'd been expecting it all. He never planned on us splitting it. Rhett was planning on the entire Lawton inheritance. Probably had been all his life.

"You were expecting all of it, weren't you?"

He laughed. "Of course. Dad had been promising it to me since I was little. He told me I was the real heir. His heir and that I deserved it. He loved me. He wanted me to have it all. This . . . bullshit about the bastard son getting it isn't fair. I'll take you to court. That will won't stand."

How had I missed this? Rhett's selfishness. I was so blinded by how much I looked up to him. But truth was, he was just like his father. He wanted everything, and he didn't care who got hurt along the way. I looked at him. Really looked at him for the first time. I didn't see the older brother who I trusted. I saw a younger version of the man who I had once called Father. When had this happened? When had he turned?

"When did you become like him?"

Rhett looked as if he didn't understand my question. He was so focused on the Lawton fortune he couldn't see anything else. It was as if I was losing him. Like the brother I had known was no more.

"Who? Dad? I've always been like Dad. Which is why I deserve what is his. What is rightfully his."

He was proud of it. Proud to be like that man. That made no sense to me. Why would anyone want that?

"You weren't like this before," I argued, trying to see if

any part of the brother I grew up loving was still there.

He rolled his eyes and tossed the ball against the wall and let it fall. "Whatever, Gunner. Just be the bastard that you are and make us take this shit to court. We will. We aren't letting the bastard son win. It's not right. That's not how it's done. You know that. You know what's right."

He was spouting off things he'd heard his father say. Things he believed. They hadn't told him the truth. His father was protecting that secret, but I knew it now. Mother had made sure to give me what I needed to win. I didn't want the money to beat them.

I wanted it to make something of it. The way the Lawtons had sat on it for years, using it as a trophy to make them lofty and important disgusted me. Especially living in the home, being treated as if I weren't worth shit. This money was mine now, and I was changing things. Country clubs and cotillions were no longer.

Not anymore.

"Are you listening to me?" Rhett taunted. "We will take you and clean you out. That's our plan. Don't fuck with us."

I didn't know who he thought "us" was, but our mother didn't want them to win. I had the power completely, and I wasn't worried.

"There won't be a court battle," I said simply.

He laughed and grinned like an idiot. "Hell yeah, there will. Dad will take you down."

If I was a bigger man, I'd walk away and let him think whatever he wanted. But I wasn't. I was a seventeen-year-old who had been talked down to and kicked around by this family my whole life. So sticking it to my brother felt like the right thing to do, as much as it hurt to do it.

"Seeing as how your father was a bastard and has no Lawton blood running through his veins, that might be a bit of a hurdle. But good luck with that and all."

I didn't wait for him to respond. I turned and walked away, only one—okay, maybe both—of my hands flipping him off on my exit.

As I walked past the door to the office I was never allowed to enter as a child or even now, I stopped and, without knocking, threw the door open. The man I hated more than anyone else on earth glared at me with a furious expression.

"Do not walk into my office unannounced or uninvited," he roared.

This time I rolled my eyes and walked over to sit on the edge of his desk. "Seeing as this here is all mine and you aren't even a Lawton, I figure I'll do whatever the hell I want."

If eyes could bulge out of your head until they

appeared to be on the verge of popping out, his just did. And I laughed. Because that was truly the funniest shit I'd ever seen.

"I'll call the police," he warned.

I reached for his phone and held it out to him. "Please do, Father dear. Please fucking do."

I Had My Own Past to Overcome

CHAPTER 45

WILLA

I could hear Nonna on the phone as she talked to her friend in Nashville, Tennessee. Every word. Part of me knew I should just start packing my bags now, but the small amount of hope I clung to kept me from doing so. This phone call meant I was leaving. The walls weren't thick, and I knew what was being said.

Nonna was trying to get me into an all-girl Catholic school where her friend worked. From the sound of things, I'd be living with her friend and cleaning her house to pay for my room and board. It wasn't as bad as a correctional center, but it was somewhere else I'd be alone.

Maybe I was meant to be alone. Life had taken any

relationships that I cherished and ripped them away from me. I was getting tough. There weren't even any tears this time.

There would be no telling Gunner bye. She'd already demanded I not speak to him or contact him. Doing so would get me sent away even faster. Nonna believed we'd been doing something wrong, and I couldn't tell her the truth. That was Gunner's secret to tell.

I would protect him and his secret however I could. This wouldn't kill me. I had survived much worse.

I stood up, walked over to my closet, and began taking the clothes down one at a time and folding them. Items I thought I wouldn't need I left here. I had nowhere else to leave them. Nonna was disappointed in me, but she wasn't banishing me forever. She was keeping me from making my mother's mistakes. She hadn't said that, but I understood it just the same.

My nonna loved me. She was in there trying to find a safe place away from all teenage boys so I wouldn't end up pregnant. That's why she was sending me to a Catholic school. This wasn't out of hate or annoyance. It was all out of love. It made it easier to accept.

When I heard her say good-bye, I stopped folding clothes and watched the door for it to open. This was it. I would be leaving and facing another new set of people. I wouldn't cry. I wouldn't cry. I wouldn't cry.

The door opened slowly, and Nonna's gaze found mine. She looked at the clothes on my bed, then back up at me. There was a sadness in her eyes, and there was worry. She was truly worried for me. I loved her for that even more. Whatever she chose to do, I would do. I wasn't fighting it.

"You're packing," she said simply as she stepped farther into the room.

I nodded. "Figured I'd be productive."

She frowned. "I don't want to send you off, Willa. I love having you here with me. You're home here, and it makes life brighter. But I can't let you down like I did your mom."

Just as I'd guessed, it was about my mom. "I know" was all I could say.

"You've got so much potential. Potential that your mother didn't have. You've got a big heart, and you know how to overcome obstacles."

The tears that I said I wouldn't cry stung my eyes.

"I love that boy. Gunner is a good boy. He's been neglected, and he's damaged because of it. But deep down he's got a heart ain't neither of his parents have. He's special, too. But he is damaged, Willa. The boy ain't ever been loved in that home. He don't know what that feels like. Close as he got was me, and I'm just the hired help. Not being loved by the people who are supposed to take care of you messes you up. I can't trust him not to ruin your life. He won't mean to, but he will. He can't be that guy for you."

She didn't know the Gunner I knew, but she had been around him more than I had. She had watched him grow, and she'd seen all his troubles. Maybe she was right. He hadn't told me he loved me, and he'd used my love against me to get his way. Was that the only way he knew how to accept love? Could I let him take a piece of my heart and not know how to protect it? I didn't have much left. Poppy and Quinn had already taken a large chunk.

"There's a girls Catholic school about two hours from here on the north side of Nashville. My friend Bernadette is the headmaster there. I've known her since she was a girl. We can't afford to pay the tuition, but you could get in on scholarship if you worked hours in the office every week before school and after school. Bernadette will let you stay in her guest bedroom and feed you if you'll do daily chores and then deep-clean on the weekend. It won't be easy, but it'll keep you busy and out of trouble."

I had already heard most of this when she'd been talking on the phone. This sounded very lonely, and my heart ached to think of leaving here again. I would miss Nonna, and Gunner and Brady. Coming back here had been my hope for healing, if that was even possible. I'd barely been here, and I was already being shipped out. When my mother had kicked me out, I'd begged her to let me stay. I had been scared. She'd ignored me. I couldn't beg again. That hurt too much.

"Okay" was all I said. Why say more?

Nonna frowned and walked over to me. When she put her hand on my shoulder, I tried not to flinch. Because even though I knew this was out of love, it still was too similar to what had just happened with my mother.

"But that idea makes me sad. I like having you here. I can't get a good feeling about sending you away, even though I know Bernadette would take care of you. So here's my other offer. Stay here with me and homeschool. I've got the Internet, and I'll get you a computer. Don't socialize with those boys and study hard. Could be that you graduate early. Get that diploma, and then we will focus on college. You've got a big world out there, Willa, and I don't want you to miss it with one mistake."

I could hear what she was saying, but I was afraid to believe her. Was this real? She was giving me an option to stay here. Even if it was basically house arrest. I wouldn't have to go to some strange place and readjust again. I could stay in my room and work here. Prove to Nonna I was as smart as she thought I was.

This meant no more Gunner, but after last night I wasn't

sure there would be anyway. Loving Gunner wouldn't save him. It hadn't changed him. He was self-destructive and angry. And loving him didn't mean I could sacrifice any more of my life for him. I had my own past to overcome.

"I want to stay here," I said. "I'll work very hard and make you proud."

She smiled and pulled me into her arms. A place I had always found peace as a child. "You already do, Willa. You already do."

She Wasn't Anything Like Willa.

CHAPTER 46

BRADY

Last night Gunner and Willa hadn't returned. I wasn't sure what was up with Rhett, but Gunner hadn't seemed surprised by his behavior. Neither had Willa, which was odd. Gunner had wanted her help too. It was almost like she knew a secret.

Pulling my truck into the Lawtons' large circular drive that went in front of the house, I noticed Gunner sitting on the top step. What the hell? I killed the engine and jumped out to go check on him. He looked like he hadn't gotten any sleep. Was Rhett on drugs or something?

"Hey, you okay?" I called out as I climbed the steps to where he was sitting. As I got closer, I noticed he was eating a bowl of cereal and had a cup of coffee beside him.

"Fucking fantastic. How are you?" was his snide response.

"Seriously, Gunner, you didn't come back last night. What happened with Rhett?"

He took a drink of his coffee, then stared up at me. "He's a selfish bastard just like his father. How's your family?" He still sounded snappy.

Most people got annoyed with him when he did this and left him alone. But I'd seen the shit inside that house and I got it. He might have all the money in the world and the power of the Lawton name, but it wasn't as easy as all that. His family was screwed up.

"Did you get any sleep?" I asked him, ignoring his question about my family.

He chuckled. "Don't I look like it?"

His hair was messy, and he had dark circles under his eyes. "Not particularly. No."

Again he laughed, then ate some more of his cereal. "Ever think of just running away from this place and not looking back?" Gunner asked.

No, I never thought of that. My parents were my biggest support system, and I had college football next year to look forward to. I shook my head no, but he already knew my response.

"Didn't figure you did. But damn if I don't want to run. Forget this town, my last name, these assholes who live in this house with me. Just leave it all."

"College is in just a few months. Our senior year will be over before we know it. Then you can leave it all behind. Start new. Get a life without them in it."

He nodded. "Yeah. That's what Willa said too. But y'all don't get how just one more day is hell. A few fucking months is a big deal. I want out now. I never want to see their faces again. Not one of them."

"Not even Rhett?"

He glowered as he stared straight ahead. "Especially Rhett."

There were things he wasn't telling me. "What's going on with Rhett? Y'all have always been close."

Gunner snarled, but there was a softness behind his anger. "No, Rhett's just always been fake. That's all. None of that was real."

"Is this about his getting drunk last night? You know college life sometimes does that to people. He was probably out at some frat party and had too many drinks and got stupid. Talk to him this morning when he sobers up."

Gunner turned his gaze to me. There was a cold emptiness there I hadn't expected. "I've talked to him sober this morning. It's even worse than last night's drunk. Don't talk about things you know nothing about, Brady. Just go back to the happy place you call home and eat your momma's pancakes with those damn blueberries and whip cream on top and have one big ole family hug. Leave the real shit here with me. I can deal with it."

Ouch. He was bitter and angry. I got it, but I was trying to help. "Talk to me, then. Explain it to me. Maybe I can help."

"You. Can't. Help. Go home, Brady. Just fucking leave me to this."

I was a good friend, and because I was a good friend I was going to leave and let him settle down and calm his shit. I couldn't help if all he wanted to do was take shots at me. I didn't give him this life. I was just trying to listen and be supportive.

"Fine. I'll go. You know where I am if you want to talk."

He gave me a sharp nod; then he stood up and walked up the stairs and into the house.

On my way back to my house I thought about stopping by Willa's and seeing what she knew but decided against it. Ms. Ames would be there, and she didn't seem too keen on me being around Willa. I didn't want to cause any trouble.

Pulling off the Lawton property, I turned right to drive through town before going to the house. See if anyone was out this early. Momma was probably making breakfast, and I would need to get back before long. I was sure West would be joining us for that too. He always did on Saturdays.

Stopping at a red light, my gaze landed on a familiar face as she walked down the street. Riley was Gunner Lawton's ex and the reason Rhett almost lost his football scholarship. She'd accused him of rape. Everyone knew Riley was a virgin. She was the typical good girl, and why she was dating Gunner, no one knew. It was only a matter of time before he cheated on her, but then the rape thing came out and . . . my eyes finally left her face to focus on the fact she was pushing a stroller.

Was she babysitting these days? Glancing down, I took in the small face of the baby girl. Her blond curls and big blue eyes looked so much like Riley's. Had her parents had a baby? I didn't really care. Riley was a lying bitch who couldn't be trusted. Why she was back in town made no sense to anyone. She wasn't wanted here. Maybe that was what was wrong with Rhett. Riley being here was causing issues at the Lawtons'. That made sense. Why didn't she just leave and let them be?

Turning my truck around, I headed home. I should have stopped and told her what a mess she was making of Gunner's home life, but she wouldn't care. She only cared about her own gain. No one else's. That was the kind of girl you ran from. She wasn't anything like Willa.

Willa was something else I had to work through in my head. I liked her. A lot. I wanted to be with her. But from the way she and Gunner had looked at each other last night and the fact he'd only let her leave with him meant something. Right now he needed someone more than I did. If Willa was helping him, then I had to stand back and let it happen.

I Have to Take Care of Me

CHAPTER 47

GUNNER

Ms. Ames was working in the kitchen when I got back inside. The smell of cheese and eggs coming from the oven meant she had a quiche going in there. That would be a hell of a lot better than my cereal had been.

"Morning, Ms. Ames," I said as I took my bowl to the sink to rinse it. When I was a kid, I had been instructed by Ms. Ames that real men didn't leave their dishes dirty in the sink. My father left his on the table for Ms. Ames to pick up. I liked the idea of being more of a man than him, so I had started cleaning my own dishes. Even if it was to one-up my dad, it made Ms. Ames happy. That was a bonus.

"Good morning," she said, not smiling in return.

I paused and studied her a minute. She seemed concerned about something.

"You okay today?" she asked.

I nodded. No use in telling her my shit. She was just the help. She didn't need to know the mess going on around her. "I'll be better when I get some of that quiche."

She didn't smile but nodded, then turned to go back to her work. I thought she was done with me when she said something else. "Willa's got some hurt deep inside like you do. She has healing to do. Let her heal."

I paused and thought about what she'd just said. I wasn't keeping Willa from healing. She had talked to me more than anyone else. I was helping her. "I know that. She talks to me."

Ms. Ames stopped what she was doing with the bowl in front of her and glanced back up at me. "Girls don't need to be sneaking out to see boys in the middle of the night. That don't lead to good things. Willa doesn't need that right now."

That's what this was about. Willa had been busted last night. Well, damn. It was times like this I really wish she had a phone like the rest of the modern world so she could text me and prepare me for this kind of thing.

"Won't happen again," I assured her, picking up a croissant and heading out the door.

"No, it won't," she agreed.

That had sounded a little forceful and matter-of-fact. Ms. Ames putting her foot down. That made me smile. I went back toward the stairs like I was going to my room but headed for the back west entrance so I could sneak over to see Willa. I needed to make sure she was okay. Ms. Ames didn't seem real happy with her. Or me.

Dealing with Brady's nosy ass this morning hadn't helped after my interaction with Rhett and his father. Rhett was currently in his father's office being told the truth. I'd started this, and now they all had to finish it. I knew the truth now. Didn't mean I still didn't want to run away, but knowing it made me feel more powerful. Not complete or a part of this family, but I still felt in control. It was the best I could do with this situation, though a part of me still ached for the family I never had, and would never have.

When I made it outside the house, I ran back near the tree house and used the wooded area for cover so no one saw me headed to Ms. Ames's house. Especially Ms. Ames. Seeing Willa and hearing her talk would make my morning better. She was the only thing that could. Once I got to the back door, I knocked and waited. After a few minutes I knocked again. Nothing.

Where could she be? Just before I walked away to go

knock on her window, a letter fell through the slot on the door and bounced on its corner when it hit the porch, before flopping on its back at my feet.

Gunner was clearly written on the front in Willa's handwriting.

"Willa? Open the door," I said loud enough so she could hear me.

Nothing.

What in the hell was going on? She was in there. Proof was at my feet in some silly letter. Bending down, I picked it up and opened it to pull out a handwritten letter folded neatly inside. "Willa! What is this about?" I called out, my heart sinking. Letters from girls who won't speak to you are never a good thing. I needed her to talk to me. I didn't need a note! Dammit!

When she said nothing, I unfolded the letter and began to read.

> *Gunner,*
>
> *I'm sorry that this has to be done in a letter. Believe me, this is not my way of being afraid to face you. It's the only way I can protect myself. Not from you but from being sent away. Again.*
>
> *Nonna was waiting on me last night*

when I got home. It didn't look good, and it was similar to what had happened with my mother when she was this age. Nonna is afraid I'll end up like my mother, and she is worried about me.

I had no one and Nonna took me in. She deserves more from me than my sneaking around. She asked me to not spend time with boys, and I broke that rule within the first week of my being here. It isn't fair to her. She is giving me a home when no one else will.

You have a lot of hurt inside you that needs time and space to heal. Going off to college next year will give you that. There's this whole world outside of Lawton that you can conquer then. I can't give you the healing you need. I'd like to think that loving you is enough, but it isn't. You can't love yet. Our timing is off, and for both of us this is better.

I'll be homeschooling the rest of the year and staying in this house. No social outings or contact with anyone. It's for the best. I need to heal too.

I'm sorry I can't be there for you, but I have to take care of me.

Willa

I didn't reread it. I didn't have to. The words were clear. I folded the paper back into the neat little rectangle it had been in and placed it back in the envelope before slipping it back through the slot.

Then I walked away. There was no reason to argue with her. I was tired of begging the world to love me. I was exhausted from trying to be good enough for someone to want to fight for. Willa was no different. I should have expected that. Something was wrong with me. That was the only explanation.

She hadn't loved me. If she loved me, she would have opened that door and faced me. Explained this to me. Given me more than a piece of paper. I had come to her house. Knocked on her door and called out her name.

That was as close to begging as I was going to do. Ever again. I should have known better than to love someone and trust them to love me in return.

CHAPTER 48

WILLA

Standing in my window, I held the letter he'd read, then slipped back to me. His retreating form was stiff, and I wanted to call out his name and run after him. But I couldn't. Nonna had made it clear I had to stay away from Gunner or I'd be going to a Catholic school in Nashville.

He hadn't said anything else to me through the door or even tried to ask me questions. I had been prepared to respond if he had. Ignoring him was too hard. It hurt me to not respond to him. The letter was the only way I could think of and not get in trouble with Nonna. She didn't understand that Gunner needed me. She was worried about me.

When I could no longer see him anymore, I set the letter on my nightstand and walked back to the kitchen where the phone was. Calling him was tempting, but it wouldn't help. It would make things harder.

So I stood there alone in the kitchen. Wishing things were different. Knowing they never would be.

Two days later Nonna had supplied me with a laptop and gotten me signed up for homeschooling online. She wasn't that great with technology, but I was, so I had been able to research it and show her what she needed to do. Monday I had thought I might get to sleep late since we weren't set up for online classes yet, but Nonna had woken me up at five in the morning with a list of things she wanted done in the house.

From before the sun rose to after it set I worked on that list. Only took a break to eat lunch. I didn't complain though. I'd much rather be cleaning Nonna's house than that of some strange woman I didn't know in Nashville.

Tuesday morning I was relieved to have my computer and classes ready so I wouldn't have to do another of those lists again. Not that there was anything left to do in this house. It was spotless and completely organized now.

However, Nonna woke me up at five again with another list, this one much shorter than yesterday's, and had me do those things before eight when she expected me to start my classes. At this rate I was going to start going to bed at eight every night in order to survive. No one should be awake at five in the morning. It wasn't even light out yet.

I was almost done with the last item on the list, mopping the back porch, when Nonna came up to the house with a worried frown.

"You talked to Gunner?"

I shook my head. "No, ma'am."

"You sure?" she asked in a more demanding tone.

"I swear. He came here Saturday morning, and I didn't answer the door. He went away. He hasn't been back."

Nonna sighed and her shoulders sagged. "This is the second morning he hasn't come down for breakfast. Yesterday morning his bed was unmade when I went to clean his room. But then I don't clean on Sundays, so that could have been since Saturday night. He didn't come get breakfast yesterday morning and this morning. When I went to make up his bed, it was untouched. Just like I left it yesterday."

"Have you called the Higgenses? Asked Brady or his mom? Maybe he's there." That was hopeful thinking. He wasn't there. He was gone. Gunner had run. Just like he wanted to. And it was my fault. I was all he had to talk to about this, and I had shut him out to save myself.

"I did." She nodded. "They ain't seen him either. I'm

gonna have to tell his momma. She's off in San Francisco at some spa."

She didn't say she needed to tell his dad. There was no point. He wouldn't care. "Is Rhett still home?"

She shook her head. "No, he left Sunday."

My heart hurt. It had taken my Nonna to notice Gunner was missing. He had known running wouldn't affect them. They wouldn't look for him. This was what he wanted. It's the only way he thought he could find happiness.

"He's run, Nonna. He hates his parents. He hates this town. So he left. He was threatening to do it that night I was at the tree house with him. He . . . he wanted me to go with him. I said no. I couldn't. I had you to think about."

Nonna stood there staring at me for several moments. Then finally she spoke. "Does that boy know, about his father?"

My nonna had been in that house for over thirty years. She knew a lot. She'd seen a lot. I just nodded.

"Who told him?"

"His mother."

She shook her head. "She told that boy, then took off to California to a spa. Jesus, it don't get no worse. Poor kid."

I swallowed the lump in my throat. Knowing Gunner was gone and alone was hard. I wanted to go after him, but I had no idea where to start or even what to say. I'd pushed him the rest of the way out the door with that letter. If I'd just opened the door and talked to him . . .

"Do you think she'll look for him?" I asked.

Nonna nodded. "He's her cash cow. That's how she sees him. She'll look for him."

I hated them all too. For hurting Gunner and treating him like he was an unwanted possession they had to keep. A part of me hated me for turning him away. Even though I was trying to stay close by doing it.

Gunner needed to find love. Maybe out there he would learn to love and find the happiness he didn't have here. If this was what he wanted, letting him go was all I could do. But I wish I could talk to him just one last time.

"Go on back inside and start your schoolwork. I'm going to go back to the big house and make some calls. See if I can't figure out where he's taken off to before I call his momma. She'll drag her heels doing it."

Nonna turned and headed back to the Lawtons'. I watched her go, thinking she'd never find him. He hadn't left without thinking about it. This had been planned, and he had the money to stay hidden.

"Be safe, Gunner," I whispered, although he was nowhere near me. Then I turned and went inside to put the mop away and begin my first day as a homeschooled senior in high school.

It Was for Both of Us

CHAPTER 49

GUNNER

I stared at the toss phone I'd bought at the local Walmart before taking off. I had left my iPhone turned off and hidden in my room. Not that I thought my parents might want to actually find me, but if they did realize I was missing, then tracking me via my cell was easy.

Although I had over ten thousand dollars in cash, thanks to my father's lack of creativity with the combination, I'd been able to take it out of the vault in the office, I was living cheap. The motel room I'd ended up at somewhere in Tennessee, about five hundred miles from Lawton, was only forty dollars a night, and it was for good cause. This place was a shit hole.

I didn't have anyone to call, so why I had gotten the phone in the first place was stupid. Last night I'd considered calling Brady or West and letting them know I was gone for good. But I hadn't.

Staring at it now, I wanted to call Willa. If anyone would be worried, it would be her. Did she even know I was gone yet? Would her Nonna tell her, since she was apparently under house arrest?

I kept going over that letter in my head. Wishing I hadn't given it back but kept it. My pride had won out that day, and I'd shoved it back at her. My pride wasn't winning out now though. I wanted to see her. Read her words. Talk to her.

God, I missed her.

Flopping back on the cheap-ass bed I was sitting on, I directed my frustrated gaze to the water-stained ceiling. Was this what I had wanted? Running across the country from one cheap motel to the next, alone? Sure didn't feel free. Not living in that house with those people was a relief, but this wasn't much better. It was lonely. Ms. Ames wasn't in the kitchen cooking, and I wouldn't get to go out on the field in the afternoons and play football.

More importantly, there was no Willa here. I should have fought harder. She'd been the one to tell me she loved me. I hadn't said the words back to her. Because I hadn't been able to. Saying those words sounded like a promise, and I wasn't good at keeping promises. I was a Lawton, after all. Blood or not, the other men that I knew that had the same last name didn't have a moral bone in their body. Why would I be different?

If I had been able to say those words, would she have opened that door Saturday? Would she have gone against the rules for me then? Had I even fucking thought about that?

No.

Growling in frustration, I pounded my fists on the bed. This wasn't what I wanted. I wanted to be . . . hell, I wanted to be a Brady Higgens or a West Ashby. A guy who Willa could trust and love without fear. A guy who could tell her he loved her back like she deserved. Why did I have to be so goddamn messed up?

Willa was the best thing that ever happened to me. When I was a little boy and now. Both times she walked into my life and gave me a reason to smile. A reason to hope for more. Running away was throwing that away. I knew there would never be another Willa. Never another chance for the way she made me feel.

But going back meant facing the demons in my house. Conquering them and learning how to live with the changes. Convincing myself I wasn't that little boy anymore who they could mistreat was tough. I still saw them as being powerful and in control.

Sitting up, I reached for my phone and dialed the only number I could right now.

It rang twice before he answered. "Hello." Brady's voice was comforting. Simply because it was a part of home. A part of Lawton. A place I thought I hated, yet my chest warmed at the idea of it. My parents weren't the town.

The town was Brady and his family, West and his mom, Asa and his family, Nash and Ryker. It was all those people I'd grown up around, and it was Ms. Ames . . . and Willa.

"It's Gunner," I said.

"Where are you, man? Coach about shit when you missed yesterday. I went by your house and no one answered. Even went by Willa's and nothing there, too. She's not at school either."

"Willa is fine. She's being homeschooled. I'm coming back. I thought I wanted to run, but I'm coming back. I need your help with something though."

He paused. "You ran? Like in away from home?"

Figures Brady was going to get hung up on all the details. I needed him to focus on what I was going to ask him. Not the play-by-play of my taking off.

"Yeah, shit got bad at home, so I just left—"

"Where are you?" He cut me off, sounding panicked now.

I smiled. I was missed. Brady missed me. I hadn't given

credit to Brady for caring when he'd tried to show me more than once he was there if I needed him. I'd just felt safe with Willa. Knowing he cared . . . that felt good. "I'm about five hundred miles away, but I'm coming home. Now would you listen to me and do something for me?"

"When did you leave? Jesus, Gunner, I tried to be a friend and listen to you on Saturday. You sent me packing. If you needed to talk, I was available. You didn't have to take off."

If Mr. Do-Gooder didn't shut the hell up and listen to me, I was going to lose my shit. "Brady, could you focus please?"

"I'm focused. What do you want? I'm going to need a good excuse for why you aren't at practice again. We need you on the field Friday night. Coach won't let you play if you don't have a good excuse."

A good excuse was the last thing on my mind. "Tell Willa to tell Ms. Ames everything. Explain it all. And that I'm coming home."

I almost added to tell her that I loved her, but I wanted to say those words myself. To her. It was for both of us. A part of my moving on and letting go of the bitterness that controlled me.

"Okay . . ." he replied slowly, then added, "Is this gonna get her in trouble? Because she's on probation. She can't get in trouble. Or is she already? Why is she home-schooled?"

"All this can be answered later. Just do it. Please."

"I'll try. Now come home."

Gunner Didn't Even Have That

CHAPTER 50

WILLA

A knock on the door broke into my studies, and I was grateful. I'd been sitting here for over four hours. This was boring. But it wasn't Catholic school.

I got up, went to the kitchen, and peeked through the window first. My mother's silver BMW was parked outside. I paused, unsure that was who I was seeing. Why would my mother be here . . . in her car?

Dropping the curtain back into place, I walked to the door slowly, trying my hardest not to panic. She had no reason to be here unannounced. I glanced at the phone and thought about calling Nonna. I wanted her here.

My mother knocked again. I had nothing to be scared

of. This wasn't my mother's house. She couldn't throw me out of here. If anything, she'd get thrown out.

Unlocking the door, I turned the brass knob with a sick knot in my stomach. I pulled it open and tried to breathe normally, but it was hard. I hadn't seen her since the day she kicked me out. I hadn't spoken to her either.

"Hello, Mom," I said simply.

"Willa. Is Mother here?" was her businesslike response.

"She's at the big house." I almost offered to call her but decided that my mother could do that herself.

"Can I come in?" she asked, and I really wanted to say *No, you can't. Leave.*

But I stepped back so she could walk inside. Mother looked around the kitchen as if expecting to find something. "It's the same. She never changes anything," Mom said, almost annoyed with that. I loved that Nonna's never changed. It was safe and familiar.

"Why are you here?" I asked, not waiting for her to get to the point. I didn't like her looking down her nose at Nonna's house. It was my home.

"To see you," Mother finally replied. She put her hand on her stomach, and I glanced down for the first time to see the small bump starting to show.

"Chance told me you were expecting another one. Congrats on that."

She smiled. "Thank you."

I hadn't actually been sincere, but she didn't catch that. Whatever.

"I came to tell you that myself and to discuss your future. I can't expect Mother to continue to take care of you."

I hadn't planned on staying here after senior year. "Senior year is almost half over. I'll be going to college after that."

Mom nodded. "About that . . ." She motioned toward the living room. "Why don't we sit down. My feet are tired, and my lower back is killing me."

I wasn't surprised she was a dramatic pregnant woman. I doubted she had gotten to be that dramatic with me at fifteen. Now she had a husband to dote on her. She had to be eating that up. I felt sorry for Chance having to witness that daily.

I followed her into the living room, and we each took a place at opposite ends of the sofa. I tucked one leg underneath me as I turned toward her.

"Okay. Talk," I said, wanting to get on with this. Suddenly my schoolwork was looking promising.

"I know you are expecting the savings account that Nonna helped me set up when you were born for your college. However, that's not going to be available. Times got tight over the years, and I wasn't always able to put money away. Then, with the new baby, I need extra money for a nursery. You're almost eighteen, Willa. It's time you make a life on your own without my help or your nonna's. Get a job and pay bills. We can't be expected to let you freeload. That won't make you a hard worker."

Nonna had put twenty thousand dollars from my grandfather's life insurance settlement into a savings account when I was born, for my college. It was supposed to have been accruing interest over the years. My mother had claimed a few times to be adding money to it, but I hadn't heard her say anything about it in years. I hadn't expected money from her, but that money Nonna had saved was going to get me through my first year while I worked and saved up for my next year. I was also going to apply for financial aid. I had this all figured out.

"Nonna put twenty grand into that account," I said, not sure what she was saying.

Mother straightened her shoulders. "That was my father's life insurance money. You needed things over the years, and money was tight often."

Wait? What? "Are you saying you spent my money?"

She glared at me. "It wasn't your money. It was my father's. He'd have wanted me to use it if I needed it. He didn't even know you."

She had spent my college money. I sat there and repeated that over and over in my head. If this was a nightmare, I'd really like to wake up now. Thank you very much.

"You need to stop living off my mother and get a real job. Make money and find your own two feet. Mom has coddled you. You've had it too easy with her, and you were spoiled and selfish and made stupid decisions that lost a little girl her life."

If she had taken a knife from the kitchen and shoved it through my chest, it wouldn't have hurt any worse right now. Being accused of Quinn's death was the most painful thing I'd ever face. Especially from my mother. I'd have never touched a drink or taken one smoke if I'd known Quinn was upstairs.

"That's not fair," I managed to choke out through the tightness in my throat. Making it hard to breathe.

"Tell that to Quinn and Poppy's parents. To that town. Tell them it's not fair, Willa. What isn't fair is that since you came into this world you've been a problem. Just like your father. Useless."

She stood up and again placed her hand on her stomach, as if protecting herself.

"I'm just glad I'm not like you," I said as she walked toward the door.

"You never were," she spit. "You even look like him."

Anger was slowly replacing my pain, and I stood up with my gaze locked on hers. "Good. Guess I got lucky then," I retorted.

She jerked her head back like I'd slapped her. "Don't you dare talk to me in such a way. I'm going to tell Mother to pack you up and send you on your way. Figure out what the real world is like. It's time you grew up, Willa."

"The only person leaving this house will be you." Nonna's voice filled the room in a loud commanding tone, and I had never been happier to hear anything in my life.

"Momma," my mother began, but Nonna held up her hand to stop her.

"Get out of my house with that evil heart and mouth of yours. That girl don't deserve this from you. Go spew your venom elsewhere. If you come back, I'll call the cops. You hear me? Leave!" Nonna pointed to the door, just in case my mother wasn't sure on the exit.

She opened her mouth to speak again, and Nonna shook her head. "I've heard enough."

"I'm pregnant! I came to tell you!" she yelled.

"I can see that. And you want money from me to support that baby. I know that, too. Leave my house now!"

My mother balled her hands into fists and stormed out of the house. Nonna slammed the door behind her. I watched as she touched the door with one hand and took a deep breath. That had to be hard on her. Nonna loved my mother. She wasn't a mother like mine was. She was loving. She wanted the best.

"I'm sorry I didn't get here sooner," Nonna finally said as she turned around to face me. "That girl is mean. Always has been. Can't for the life of me figure out where her meanness comes from. Her daddy was a good man."

"She used all my college money," I told her. That was the one thing that was said I couldn't shake loose. It affected everything.

Nonna nodded. "I know. I checked on it over the years and saw she was taking some a little at a time. I began to do the same. I ended up saving about seven thousand of it. I added it to my savings account that has the rest of your grandfather's life insurance money in it, and that is more than enough to get you through college. You'll need a job of course to pay for your food and extras, but the classes will be paid for and the dorm."

"She doesn't know you took some?" I asked, still in a daze going from being told I had no college money to being told I had enough for all of my college.

"Your mother isn't smart with money. She can't afford a new baby, yet she's driving around in a flashy foreign car. I figured I needed to take care of your future, because she's only worried about hers."

Tears filled my eyes, and I didn't hold them back. I let them freely roll down my face as I closed the distance between me and my nonna. Having a mother like mine was hard. But I had my nonna.

Gunner didn't even have that.

Nonna pulled me into her arms and held me tightly. I sobbed against her chest for the mother I didn't have, the grandmother I did have, and the life Gunner had been given.

The Good Lord Wasn't Going to Swoop down and Change Anything

CHAPTER 51

GUNNER

I walked back into my house after several hours on the road with a plan. This was my home, and I was making it somewhere I wanted to come back to. I headed to the office, where I'd last spoken to the man who wasn't my father.

Without knocking, I walked inside and faced him. I didn't give him time to speak. "Next month after my birthday, you'll need to find another house to live in. You can take Mother with you. Your allowance will end. Prepare to get a job." I turned and started to walk out of the office.

"You can't do that! You have no idea how to run the Lawton holdings. You've not been trained."

"I'll hire help. I don't need you."

"You can't do this!"

"You have no Lawton blood. Yes, I can," I reminded him. "Now go quietly, or I'll make sure the town knows exactly how fucked-up this family tree is."

"You would have to tell them that you're a bastard too! It would ruin your name as much as mine."

I laughed then because he seriously thought that mattered. "They already think I'm a bastard. I'm not worried about giving them proof."

"Your mother thinks she can tell you all this and get away with it. I'll fight you on this. I won't go down easy."

"Don't really care," I replied, then walked out on his ranting. I was going to turn his office into a gym. I'd like having a good gym in the house. We should really already have had one of those.

My mother was walking inside with her designer clothes and new hairstyle as I came back down the stairs. "Hello, son. How have things been since I've been gone?"

"Fantastic, Mother," I replied, just as haughty as her.

"Ms. Ames left a message for me at the spa. Something about you not coming home. My flight was this morning so I didn't bother calling back. I would be here soon enough."

I nodded as if that was completely understandable. "Of course. One doesn't need to be bothered by a missing child. If you'll excuse me."

She gave me a confused look, and I realized she was just that shallow. I wasn't sure she had even been raped. It sounded more like a story to make her look better. She'd have slept with whoever she needed to in order to live this Lawton lifestyle.

"Has Rhett left?" she called after me.

"If there is a God," I replied.

Then I walked into the hallway leading to the kitchen. The smells of dinner were wafting from the door, and I was ready for real food. My fast-food lifestyle the past two days had been rough.

"Ms. Ames, I'm home," I said as I entered the kitchen. Her head snapped up, and a relieved smile touched her lips as if she was truly glad to see me.

"Thank the good Lord. I've been worried sick about you."

"I heard you called to tell Mother, but she couldn't be bothered calling back. She told me as much out in the entryway just now. She's home too," I explained, trying to sound as casual about the whole thing as possible.

Ms. Ames's immediate frown made me feel even more cared about. She didn't want me to feel unwanted by my parents.

"Is Willa home?" I asked.

She continued to frown. "She is. But she's homeschooling right now and can't take visitors."

"Visitors? Or just me?" I pushed.

Ms. Ames put the knife down that she'd been using to chop the vegetables. "Willa is much like you. Her mother isn't a mother to her. She's been hurt just like you have. Teenage girls go looking for love in places that end badly for them. She has a future ahead of her and getting stuck in Lawton as a single mom is not in those plans. I'll protect her from that even if I have to send her off to an all-girls Catholic school to do it."

Whoa. Whoa. Wait up. No sending her off. "I know that. I'd never do anything to hurt her. I love her." The words had come out so easily I had surprised myself.

"Sex and love ain't the same thing, Gunner Lawton," she said to me, wagging her finger.

I nodded. "I agree. Seeing as how I've never had sex with Willa. Friday night she was at the tree house with me because my mother had just told me not only am I my grandfather's son but he raped her and my pretend father was a bastard kid too and wasn't even a damn Lawton. I had a lot unloaded on me and needed someone I could trust to listen to me. That was why I asked Willa to sneak out and go to the tree house with me."

Ms. Ames's face went slightly pale. "Mr. Lawton ain't a Lawton? Good Lord. That's not stuff a boy needs to hear."

It was obvious Brady had never told Ms. Ames what I'd asked him to. She was just now hearing all this for the first time.

I disagreed. "I'll be eighteen next month, and this will all be mine. He and my mother will be moving out and finding a place of their own. Things are changing. But more importantly . . . Willa. I need to see her."

Ms. Ames sat down in the chair closest to her. "Good Lord, good Lord," she repeated, shaking her head.

The good Lord wasn't going to swoop down and change anything. The sex had been had and the babies had been made many years ago. It was all a done deal.

"Can I see Willa?"

Finally she lifted her gaze to mine. "Her mother was here. Upset her and she's resting. Give her some time before you go looking for her. She needs to make up her own mind what's good for her. I guess I can't save her from everyone. Not if she don't need saving."

I could accept that. As much as I wanted to run over there and make sure she was okay, I would give her some time. But not too much. Willa had saved me. She showed me how to love and took me from the self-destructive path I was on. Without her in my life, I'd be a wreck right now. In life you face obstacles, and you have to fight through them. If you're lucky enough, you find someone to fight for you, too. I was lucky.

Meet Me at the Tree House

CHAPTER 52

WILLA

I had just walked out of the kitchen when something hit the floor. It wasn't loud, but it still made a noise. Stopping, I turned and looked back. There was a letter by the door. Walking over to it, I set my plate of food down on the table, then bent to pick up the envelope. My name was written on the outside. It was Gunner's handwriting.

I didn't open it but jerked open the door to see if it was him. But there was no sign of anyone. I was barefoot and in my pajama pants and tank top, but I didn't care. I ran outside, still holding the letter and scanning for any sign of Gunner. Nonna had told me she would let me know the moment she heard something about him.

"Gunner!" I called out his name, but there was no one.

Frustrated, I opened the letter while standing out in the grass alone.

Willa,

Running isn't as fun without you. It's lonely. I missed home because home was where you were. When you told me you loved me, I already knew how I felt about you. I'm pretty sure I felt it when we were kids. I just didn't understand it. The whole emotion was foreign to me.

I'm home. Where I belong. With you.

Meet me at the tree house.

Gunner

I didn't put the letter back in the envelope, and I didn't think about the Catholic school. All I could think about was getting to Gunner. Seeing him and knowing he was okay. So I ran. Sticks bit into the bottoms of my feet, but I didn't seem to notice. I just had to get to that tree house.

I tucked the letter in my pants and climbed the ladder to the top, anxious to see him. To tell him I was sorry. I shouldn't have just given him a letter. He deserved more.

His eyes were the first thing I saw when I stepped

inside, and a small smile stretched across his face.

"You look beautiful. I especially like the messy hair," he said, taking in my outfit. Homeschooling didn't require I brush my hair or put on decent clothing.

"You're back" was all I could say.

He nodded. "I am."

"I'm sorry," I blurted out.

"I love you" was his response. "I have forever. I just didn't understand it until you came back into my life and completed me again."

"Oh." I wanted to say more, but I hadn't been expecting him to say that. He caught me off guard.

"Yeah, oh," he agreed with a chuckle, then closed the space between us and pulled me against him.

He held my face in his hands. "My life is fucked up, but I have one thing to promise you, and it's that you'll have my heart until the day I die. That might sound cliché and silly, but I mean it. I can't be happy without you. You are my happy."

"You're mine too."

He leaned in to kiss me, and I held on to his arms to keep from falling. A kiss from Gunner Lawton made me weak in the knees. And that was something I knew would never change.

Six years ago . . .

GUNNER

It made my chest get sharp pains and my stomach feel funny when Willa cried. I'd do anything to make her stop. I hated her tears. I just wanted her happy. I didn't know her momma, but I hated her. She was making Willa cry, and I didn't know why.

I put my arm around her small shoulders. I always felt so big compared to her little body. We were the same age, but she wasn't a big girl. She was the shortest girl in our sixth-grade class. She was also the prettiest.

"Don't cry, Willa. Just tell me what's wrong, and I'll fix it." I wasn't sure I could fix anything, but I wanted to and I'd do my best to try.

She shook her head and leaned into me. That felt good. She trusted me, and I liked that. "You can't. No one can," she sobbed.

This had to be really bad. If her nonna couldn't fix it, then what was it? Was her nonna sick? Was she fired and no one had told me?

"I can try," I said gently.

She turned her face into my chest and cried harder. "No . . . you can't. My momma is coming to get me," she said between sobs. "I haveto move away."

I was a boy and boys weren't supposed to cry, but hearing those words, I felt like crying too. Willa couldn't leave me. She was my best friend. We did everything together. She was the first person I thought of when I woke up every day.

"You can't leave," I said with more force than intended.

She pulled back and wiped at her wet face. "I have to. Nonna said my momma wants me and it's time we were a family."

No. No. Nonononono. I shook my head. "You've got a family here. With your nonna and me."

She nodded her head in agreement and continued wiping at her face. "I know. I told her that, and Nonna hugged me and told me she loved me but that my momma needed me now and Chance needs me."

Chance was her little brother she never got to see. I felt

guilty for not wanting her to get to live with him. I had my brother in my house, and it was great. She missed Chance, and when she talked with him on the phone, she always cried when they hung up. I would spend hours telling her jokes to make her smile again.

"Chance can move here," I said, thinking that sounded like a good plan.

Willa sniffled, but her sobs were slowly calming down. "He can't. His dad and my mom got married. They want to bring me there to be part of their family."

"In Arkansas?"

She nodded.

"That's so far away," I said, letting my own sorrow start to take over.

She began sobbing again, and I realized I was making it worse, not better. I didn't want to lose Willa, but if there was no choice and she had to go, I didn't want her to be sad, either. I could cry alone in my room after she was gone. But I wanted to know she was smiling and happy.

"You'll still get to visit your nonna and me. It won't be forever. And when you're older, you can come stay the whole summer here. I bet they'd let you do that if you just ask them."

Willa stopped sobbing and looked at me with hopeful eyes. "Do you think so?" she asked.

I nodded. "Sure! Your nonna will be missing you, and you'll get to come whenever you want. It's not forever."

She gave a smile then. It was still a sad one, but it was better than tears.

"We'll always be here for each other. You can come back and watch me play football at the high school on the big field under the lights." That was my dream, and Willa knew it. To play under the lights at the big stadium with Brady, West, Asa, Ryker, and Nash. We would win State, and Willa would be there cheering me on. We had snuck off a few times and walked to the high school just to stand there under the lights. All of us. We made our plans and built our dreams. In all those dreams, Willa was there.

"I wouldn't miss it. I'll be back. I won't even be gone long before I visit. We will be fine."

I wasn't sure my heart agreed. It was hurting while I was smiling. Willa was my favorite part about life. She made things better by just smiling. Her laugh could completely fix my bad mood. When no one else was around to understand, Willa did. The day I caught her playing in my tree house had been the luckiest day of my life. What would I do without her?

Acknowledgments

A big thank-you to my editor, Jennifer Ung. This was our first book together, and she was cheering me on when there were times I wasn't sure I could write a book I loved as much as *Until Friday Night*. With her encouragement, I did. I owe her for that. Also, I want to mention Mara Anastas, Jodie Hockensmith, Carolyn Swerdloff, and the rest of the Simon Pulse team for all their hard work in getting my books out there.

My agent, Jane Dystel. She's there for me when I'm having a hard time working on a story, when I need to vent, and even if I just need a recommendation on a good place to eat in New York City. I'm thankful to have her on my side.

When I started writing, I never imagined having a group of readers come together for the sole purpose of supporting me. Abbi's Army, led by Danielle Lagasse and Vicci Kaighan, humbles me and gives me a place of refuge. When I need my spirits lifted, these ladies are there. I love every one of you.

Last but certainly not least: my family. Without their support, I wouldn't be here. My three kids are so understanding, although once I walk out of that writing cave, they expect my full attention, and they get it. My parents, who have supported me all along. Even when I decided to write steamier stuff. My friends, who don't hate me because my writing is taking over. They are my ultimate support group, and I love them dearly. And, JBS, you've made my writing stronger and given me fresh, new ideas.

My readers. I never expected to have so many of you. Thank you for reading my books. For loving them and telling others about them. Without you, I wouldn't be here. It's that simple.